D0522639

Complications

Clare Jayne

DEDICATION

This book is dedicated to my mother and sister for their unwavering support.

CONTENTS

ACKNOWLEDGMENTS

I am very grateful to Wendy White, Jenny Taylor and author Lindsay Barnard for their help in proofreading this novel. A big thank you to my friends, particularly everyone on my Facebook page, for all their supportive comments. Thank you as well to the librarians at Nairn Library for being so helpful in finding and ordering books for providing background information.

CHAPTER ONE

"I AM ENGAGED," LOTTIE told her best friend. "Mr Saverney has asked me to marry him!"

Five minutes before this announcement Amelia had been in an excellent mood. She had just put on a ball gown of cream muslin over her carefully arranged black curls and Walker, her maid since birth, exclaimed, "You must be the loveliest lassie ever to have been born."

Amelia preened a bit at these words and imagined all the men at the forthcoming ball taking one look at her and instantly falling in love. Yes, everything would soon turn out as she had always planned: she would marry a wealthy, powerful man and have all of Scotland at her feet. England too - she could not wait for her first visit to London.

"Now where can Miss Harrington have got to," Walker said, doing up the buttons at the back of the gown. "It's not like her to be late."

"No, it is not," Amelia said, frowning. Lottie should have been here an hour ago as they had planned to get ready for the ball together. "I hope she is not ill. It would be terrible for her to miss the ball."

Lady Treeton held some of the best events of the season. It was the start of February and Edinburgh had only had a couple of less selective dances and the odd dinner party. All the best of society should be at the ball tonight and Amelia was keen to meet some new people.

She heard footsteps coming up the stairs then Lottie knocked twice and burst into the bedroom with her grand announcement.

She was glowing with happiness and Amelia could not help but smile in return but her first thought was that Lottie would be married first. Lottie had never done anything before Amelia so it was a considerable shock. *But I'm so much prettier…* Amelia thought despairingly. *And she'll have such beautiful new clothes…*

"Why, there are tears in your eyes," Lottie said. "You must not think for a moment that this will lessen our friendship because nothing in the world could do that."

With these words she moved forward to embrace Amelia, who hugged her back. She managed a smile as they drew apart. "This is the most wonderful news. It is an excellent match."

Their parents were waiting so there was no time for further conversation. Lottie had already dressed for the ball so Walker fixed her hurriedly prepared curls while she and Amelia both put on their gloves, then they were ready to go downstairs and leave in the carriages with their families, Lottie talking about the proposal the entire way.

As soon as they arrived at the ball Mr and Mrs Harrington, Lottie's parents, joined at once by Mr Saverney and his mother, told everyone about the engagement. After this everyone was so busy congratulating them that Amelia was entirely ignored. It was a new experience for her and not one she liked in the least.

She observed the group as her mother conversed with two other ladies. Lottie's fiancé was attractive and had charming manners. He also had an easy-going manner which suited Lottie. Amelia herself required a man with political ambition and more of a presence than Saverney possessed but there was no denying that it was the best match imaginable for her. Lottie's family were highly respectable but had little money whereas Saverney, also from a good family of course, was extremely wealthy. In conclusion, Lottie could scarcely have chosen better, even without factoring love into the matter.

His mother was perhaps his greatest drawback. She was a formidable woman, used to getting her own way, who had an opinion on every subject and was not always tactful in expressing it.

Amelia's only real concern for Lottie's future was that if she was unable to stand up to Mrs Saverney she could end up constantly being told what to do, as was currently the case with Lottie's controlling parents.

If Mrs Saverney insisted on imposing her sense of fashion on Lottie then it would be a sorry thing indeed. The gown and turban her ladyship were wearing of such luridly clashing colours and of such an ugly style that it pained Amelia to look at them.

Amelia realised Mrs Saverney had caught her stare so she had no choice but to approach with her best smile fixed in place and say politely, "We are all so pleased about the engagement, Mrs Saverney. Mr Saverney and Miss Harrington seem to me an ideal couple."

"Just so, Miss Daventry. I am more than satisfied at the prospect of Miss Harrington as a daughter-in-law."

What high praise! Amelia wondered if Lottie remotely returned the sentiment.

After a few more minutes of engagement exclamations Amelia was growing irritable. She knew she was being selfish but this was her second season - she was running out of time to marry. Admittedly her first season had been conducted largely as an observer and her father had made it clear he would not consider offers for her hand in marriage as he considered fifteen years of age too young to marry, but that was beside the point. She had not yet met anyone she felt she could love but felt she was practical enough to be willing to lower her expectations sufficiently to consider any man who was wealthy, of good character and family, attractive, devoted to her and had an important political career so they could regularly spend time in London. Surely that was little to ask?

She had been hoping to be rescued from the dull conversations with elderly ladies and fate answered her in cruel fashion with the arrival of the Duke of Elborough. He approached her with a predatory smile and bowed. She responded with a polite curtsy, thinking hastily for a way to escape.

"Miss Daventry, how charming you look. May I request the pleasure of your next dance?"

"How kind, Your Grace. Alas, I am already promised for it. Perhaps later in the evening."

She curtsied again and hurriedly sought out Lottie's brother who was standing looking tall and wistful, as though imagining himself somewhere he would like better. He was only a year older than Lottie, who had a slight tendency to mother him, so he sometimes seemed more like her younger brother, or he had done a year ago before his growth spurt and before he gave up sulking. Amelia tended to treat him like a brother of her own. He gave a half-hearted bow to Amelia who responded to it then said, "Mr Harrington, you are dancing with me. Now."

His lip curled. "I do not…"

"… Dance well. Yes, I know. However, it is you or the Duke of Elborough."

There was no arguing with this so he gave in with bad grace: "Oh, very well."

They took their places, she in the line of female dancers, he with the men. Lottie moved to her side, Saverney opposite, then the musicians began to play. Mr Harrington was, in fact, a perfectly adequate dancer; he simply disliked the pastime. Amelia found this difficult to understand as she could think of few more enjoyable ways to spend an evening.

When the music finished she accepted invitations from a couple of young gentlemen for later dances then caught Elborough looking in her direction again and moved to join the discussion her father was having with several men. It was a necessary retreat.

The Duke of Elborough whipped his horses to destruction, threatened his friends and had killed any number of men in duels. One shuddered to think how he would treat a wife. He was also, unfortunately, the only gentleman who currently seemed likely to ask for Amelia's hand and while it was pleasant to have caught the attention of a member of the peerage, she wished he would pay her less interest.

Even her father had asked her into his study to warn her off the Duke the previous year, letting her know about his bad character. She had responded with a few stories she had heard from Lottie's brother and they had both shaken their heads and agreed that it would be best if no sane woman agreed to marry the Duke.

And speaking of men no sane women should marry. Mr Brightford and his two companions bowed to her and she curtsied, thinking that there had never been a man less aptly named than Mr Brightford. She gathered it was fashionable for men to behave in a sardonic manner but he took the behaviour to extremes, permanently looking either bored or critical. Worse still, many of the younger men, for some inexplicable reason, admired him and copied this behaviour.

After a frowning glance at Amelia, Mr Brightford continued speaking to the group: "I have received a letter informing me that my cousins will visit this summer so I expect they will convince me to hold more balls and dinner parties than usual."

"More than none, sir?" Amelia said before she could stop herself. "How pleasant."

His eyes narrowed and he gave her a condescending smile. "In fact I often hold dinner parties. I simply do not invite children to him."

Her father hastily spoke before she could respond to this piece of gross impertinence. "I do not believe we have had the pleasure of meeting your cousins."

"They have an estate in England so they do not often have the opportunity to visit."

"Have they been to London?" Amelia asked eagerly, this information casting the visit in an entirely new and far more favourable light.

He looked down his nose at her with another slight frown. "Yes, of course."

Unpleasant man. She had met him the previous season and it was the only time society had disappointed her. His expression looked always to find fault and he seemed inexplicably immune to her beauty. Still, there was nothing likeable about him so she told herself it was no loss.

As soon as Lottie was free from her parents and Mr Saverney, Amelia joined her and they went in search of drinks to refresh themselves.

"I am quite embarrassed by so much attention," Lottie confessed, looking flushed and a little uncomfortable. "But everyone has been so kind in offering their congratulations."

"It is hardly kindness. You will be a very important member of society as Mrs Saverney."

Lottie's eyes widened at the thought and Amelia realised with amazement that this had not occurred to her. It would have been Amelia's first thought. "I suppose you are right. I hope I can do well. You will help me, will you not?"

Amelia smiled. "In planning balls and grand dinner parties? Nothing could give me greater pleasure." She caught side of Lottie's brother and said, "Mr Benjamin Harrington does not look much entertained this evening. Does he have any new, er, interests?"

Mr Harrington had the habit of developing romantic affections for men. The subject was utterly unspeakable, therefore Amelia and Lottie conversed upon it frequently and at length.

"Luckily, no, although I fear Mr Duneton may be here with his new fiancée."

"Is he still not speaking to Mr Harrington?"

"No. Benjy is heart-broken. He will not say exactly what happened but he clearly gave away his feelings and, as always, lost another friend."

When Mr Harrington had a tendre it was unfortunately obvious: he tended to blush, stutter and gaze at the object of his interest with puppy-like adoration. "There must be a man somewhere who could return his feelings."

Lottie bit her lip. "Father desires him to marry."

"No! I thought it had always been understood that he would remain a bachelor and adopt your first child as his heir?"

"I think he would prefer that - he considers that it would be too unfair on any woman to marry her. Our father, however, insists that it is his duty to do so and to find someone quickly. Poor Benjy does not seem to appeal to women, though."

They both turned to look at Mr Harrington who was standing with several young women and their mothers, looking bored and a bit disdainful, an expression Amelia felt sure he had adopted from Mr Brightford. "Inexplicable," she said with fond amusement. "Still, I imagine there are women who would accept such a situation. Not ladies like us, of course, who sensibly expect to be showered with adoration and gifts by the men fortunate enough to be our husbands…"

"I expect no such thing!"

"… but a less wealthy, less discriminating woman might be glad to marry Mr Harrington. I do think he must tell her the truth about himself, though, however awkward the conversation, so that she might make an informed decision."

Lottie played with the lace on her fan, frowning. "My

father would not agree but I think you are right. It would be cruel not to let her know the truth before they married."

Their conversation ended abruptly at the announcement of the - albeit late - arrival of His Royal Highness Prince William Frederick, Duke of Gloucester and Edinburgh. The attendance of so grand a figure ensured that Lady Treeton's ball would be discussed admiringly for months. His Royal Highness was wearing his bright army clothes and while his excessive weight and protruding eyes made him far from attractive, Amelia approved of his well-known opinions on the abolition of slavery and very much wanted to meet him. Not half an hour later her father approached to say that the prince wished to be introduced to her. She felt a little nervous meeting a member of the royal family but he responded to her father's introduction by saying warmly, "I see Scotland has enough beauty to rival England."

She ventured to say that she agreed with his public views against slavery and he seemed delighted and spoke to her for some while about his political beliefs and about the war against Napoleon. Lady Treeton then led him away to make further introductions but Amelia could not help but feel flattered at the meeting.

"His Royal Highness is usually not much of a ladies' man," Mr Brightford commented, appearing from nowhere at her side, "but you seem to have won him over."

Although the words should have been a compliment he said them in an insulting manner she took exception to. "Contrary to your own endeavours, sir, I do my best to be likeable."

She watched that barb sink in then turned and sauntered away.

The rest of the evening passed pleasantly with plenty of dancing, yet even after the great victory of her meeting with His Highness, Prince William, Amelia began to feel despondent when she had returned home. As Walker helped her change out of her ball gown, she said, "Why has no man asked me to marry him yet? What is wrong with them all?"

"You have put off a couple of gentlemen who showed an interest in you last year," her maid reminded her.

Amelia snorted at this. "They do not count. They had little wealth, no ambition and were not even particularly interesting. Even the Duke of Elborough would seem attractive compared to any of them."

"Don't even jest about such a thing, Miss Amy. That man is a monster."

Elborough was coarse, brutish and unpleasing to the eye, but he was at least a Duke... No, even in a daydream he was not someone she could consider but it was just wrong that Charlotte Harrington was engaged. No, that was unfair. Lottie was pretty, demure and kind as well as being the most loyal and constant of friends. She deserved the best of husbands. It was just that Amelia should have been engaged first. With her black hair and blue eyes, Amelia had always caught the attention of men and it should have been easy to make one of them fall in love with her. Amelia had planned her entire future - including how to find and captivate the right gentleman - so how had Lottie, who planned nothing, fallen into such an excellent match?

As Amelia settled down in her bed she told herself that no one else in Edinburgh that evening had drawn the interest of a prince. And it was just like Mr Brightford to try to ruin her moment of glory!

CHAPTER TWO

AMELIA AWOKE in a good mood then remembered that Lottie was engaged while she herself was not and the day was ruined.

As Walker helped her dress she said, "Perhaps I should do as Mama always tells me and try to be more demure." It was a depressing idea and something she did not think she would be good at, but the situation was desperate. In the autumn her family would leave for their country estate where she had known the people all her life and there was not an acceptable, eligible gentleman among them. Besides, as much as she loved their home, it had been built in the medieval era when apparently no one felt the cold. The thought of returning endlessly to so freezing an establishment with no prospect of a husband and no new clothes... it was not to be borne.

"Without wanting to disagree with Mrs Daventry, no, lassie. If you pretend to be demure then you'll attract men who want a demure wife and they won't be happy when they discover the deception. However, if you show men your true nature then you'll attract men who want an intelligent, strong-willed wife and will love you as you should be loved."

"That is wise, Walker," Amelia said, happy to accept that no change in her behaviour was necessary after all.

She walked downstairs to breakfast in better spirits that were once again crushed by yet more talk of the engagement and an admonishment by her mother. "Miss Harrington is a sweet child but, of course, your father and I had hoped that you would be married first."

Amelia forced a smile but was saved from answering when her father looked up from his paper and said, "However, if a man worthy enough to claim your hand has not yet made your acquaintance then we would certainly not wish you to settle for any lesser creature."

She laughed and leaned round the table to kiss his cheek. "Oh, I would never do that." She resumed her meal for a few minutes then recalled a grievance: "How dare he call me a child."

"Who said this?" Mrs Daventry asked.

"Mr Brightford, the loathsome man."

Mr Daventry commented, "You did make a somewhat impertinent remark to him first as I recall."

"What manner of remark?" Mrs Daventry demanded.

Amelia failed to mention that she had in fact insulted Mr Brightford twice during the previous evening, only describing what she had said on the earlier occasion, concluding, "It may have been a trifle impertinent but it was entirely true. The man is unsociable, bad tempered and tiresome."

"He is also a highly respected gentleman," Mrs Daventry said, "and it is certainly not for a young unrelated girl like you to speak to him in that fashion. You will not gain a husband through such sharp comments."

Amelia snorted. "I will certainly never marry Mr Brightford."

"But other gentlemen likely heard your comments and you might gain a reputation for rudeness. In the future I suggest you think carefully about what you wish to say and if it cannot be something polite then remain silent. Also, young ladies do not snort."

"Sorry, Mama." Amelia feigned a meek expression, inwardly blaming Mr Brightford entirely for the unpleasant conversation.

* * *

Benjamin Harrington sought for something to say to his future brother-in-law as they waited in the drawing room for Lottie to change into a riding outfit. Mother had decreed the velvet curtains be opened for the occasion, risking sunlight fading the colours of the fabrics for the opportunity to show her future son-in-law their smartest room at its best. Benjamin did not think Saverney had noticed; he seemed twitchy, presumably impatient to see his fiancée. "Our family is very happy about the engagement."

"So is my mother," Saverney said quickly then fell into silence, looking down to straighten the tailcoat of his elegant outfit.

Benjamin was about to ask which horses Saverney had brought to draw his phaeton then remembered that the man had no knowledge of horses. After a casual acquaintanceship of several years, he had still found nothing that they had in common. Saverney was uninterested in horses, running an estate or prize-fighting; Saverney apparently liked balls, gambling and took an interest in the latest fashions, all of which Benjamin found rather boring. He was spared having to wrack his brain further by his sister's arrival, her smile to them both radiant.

"Forgive me for keeping you waiting, Mr Saverney," she said to her fiancé.

He had jumped to his feet and bowed to her. "It is more than worth it to see you looking so lovely."

She flushed and, although her carriage dress was not

the most up-to-date or stylish, and although she would never be Miss Daventry's equal for looks, her current joy gave her a true beauty.

The two of them took their leave of Benjamin, who watched them go and wished the thought of a conventional future could bring him such joy. Lottie was the kindest of sisters and it was good to see her so happy. However, he would miss her when she left the family home. In fact, the thought of being left alone with his parents was an unpleasant one.

He had once thought he had an affectionate relationship with them, but since telling them the truth about his nature they seldom spoke to him and made it clear that they still expected him to marry, no matter how little he or presumably the woman involved could possibly want it. After Lottie's marriage perhaps they would see reason and he could go and live quietly on their country estate. The more time he spent in the city the more a reclusive life appealed to him; at least there he could throw himself into work and forget about his attractions to men instead of being rebuffed and disliked time after time.

Thoughts of the countryside reminded him of a letter he wanted to write to the family's estate manager about a tenant who was having difficulties paying the rent. The woman was recently widowed, husband and son both lost to consumption, so he had no intention of seeing her and her remaining children starve. Hopefully the estate manager would not mention the matter to Benjamin's father who let him deal with tenant matters but would not approve of losing any rent. Benjamin walked into the library and sat down with quill, ink and parchment to compose the note. As he was finishing this a maid announced Miss Daventry's arrival.

He stood up as Amelia marched in and bowed to her. She responded with a curtsy, although she rolled her eyes as she did so then gave him an impish smile. He returned it, glad of the company of one of the few people he could be entirely open with, and skipped any more formalities, saying, "Lottie is not here at present. She is riding in the park with Saverney."

She paused with a frown, clearly having expected to find Lottie at home, but what she said was, "You do not like Mr Saverney?"

His tone must have given him away - he did not have a high opinion of the man but did not have anything against him, so he could only shrug. He had not felt at first that Saverney returned Lottie's adoration, but the marriage proposal settled that. It would be pleasant to find him less tedious, but perhaps that would change in time. "He does not have the standing in society that my father might have wished for but he is wealthy and comes from a good family. Anyway, Lottie loves him so I am happy for her that he returns her feelings."

Amelia put a gloved hand on his arm, expression sympathetic, and he realised she was thinking of his own difficulties. He felt a surge of fondness for her.

When Lottie had said she had told her best friend about his romantic inclinations, Benjamin had been appalled. They had known each other since infancy but, given the behaviour of the friends to whom he had revealed the truth, he had expected Amelia to cut him out of her life. Instead, while never directly mentioning the subject, she had shown a quiet support that meant a lot to him, particularly when his own parents treated his nature as an evil affliction that must be hidden at all costs.

If only there was a rule book to tell him how to live his life. Surely he was not the only man in the world who felt romantically for other men instead of women. Was he?

* * *

Amelia's day was not improved by finding Lottie away from home at a time they had agreed to meet and she had the unpleasant feeling that Saverney would always be her friend's priority from now on and that Amelia would come a poor second. Her life was rapidly changing and not in the pleasant way she had always envisaged.

She had her carriage take her home, arriving just in time as her mother was about to leave for some charitable meeting, resplendent in a blue and purple walking dress with an elaborate feathered hat, and would need the carriage. Unfortunately, the family finances were such that they only had one equipage. On impulse, and able to think of nothing better to do, Amelia offered to accompany her mother.

"How kind of you," Mrs Daventry said with a sceptical glance.

The morning was in fact not as dull as she would have expected and it was nice to spend some time with her mother. Amelia had, of course, been raised by a nurse then a governess so she had generally not seen her parents for more than several hours a week growing up. It was only in the last year that she had begun to know them and that would likely change when she married. So it was quite pleasant to spend some time with her mother as an adult. Amelia made some suggestions at the meeting which were well received by some of Edinburgh's most influential ladies and she returned home feeling virtuous and a little smug.

It was this mood which prompted her to retire to her bedroom to work on an embroidered cushion cover which would be a birthday present for her father. The work was more than a little tedious so, after half an hour or so, she was happy to be interrupted by a quiet knock on her door.

Lottie entered the room, a worried frown marring her gentle expression. "Benjy said that you called to see me earlier - I had entirely forgotten we had arranged it. Can you forgive me?"

Amelia smiled as she put down the embroidery and rose to her feet. "Of course I can. It is of no consequence."

They embraced and Lottie said, "It will never happen again, I promise."

"Then let us change the subject. How is Mr Saverney today?"

Lottie beamed as they crossed the room to sit on chairs beside the window. "He is wonderful, so kind and attentive. His mother suggested that we have the wedding within the next three months, perhaps as soon as next month. Is it not excellent that she and Mr Saverney feel the same as I and do not want to wait?"

It seemed a little strange to Amelia but she dismissed her surprise and said, "Then you will still have a spring wedding. That could not be better."

"Indeed. Mr Saverney suggested either London or Paris for our honeymoon. What do you think?"

Amelia frowned, thinking of the changes that the French Revolution had brought about, the deaths and those fleeing the country, then the aftermath with everyone who had ever expressed a remotely liberal view being charged with sedition and transported to Australia. "With the war so bad, I would not have thought France was a safe place to visit just now, but of course I am not an expert on the subject. I should think London would be wonderful. It has the best modistes in the country and, of course, you must buy a whole new wardrobe."

"Even with a new wardrobe of clothes I could never look as beautiful as you," Lottie said in a comforting way and Amelia realised her words must have sounded wistful.

She smiled brightly, putting the thought of elegant afternoon outfits and stunning ball gowns from her mind. "Clearly Mr Saverney thinks you more beautiful than anyone else."

Lottie blushed and laughed. "Perhaps. It still seems unbelievable that he can love me as much as I love him. I will try so hard to be the best wife possible to him."

"He is the one who is lucky and should strive to

deserve you, but as he regularly expresses his admiration for you he seems to be aware of his good fortune, which is in his favour. Do you know when you will visit his country estate or how much time he intends you to spend there?"

"He did not mention it. I will ask."

"You must not forget that once you are married you will be mistress of the estate. You must not defer to Mrs Saverney."

"But, Amelia, how can I not?" Lottie exclaimed "She has been in control of both households all of her married life. It would not be fair for me to start contradicting her orders."

"That is what happens when women marry, although I do understand your concern. Naturally you would not want to offend her but you must not be too meek and let her make decisions about your life." Mrs Saverney was strong-willed and Lottie was just the opposite. It would be unfair if Lottie were forced into constant obedience the way she always had been by her parents. "If you make a stand at the outset it will be easier later."

"I think she likes me…"

"… Of course she does!"

"… So I am sure we can arrange things to satisfy us both."

Amelia was not so certain but they could worry about that later. "Have you any ideas for your wedding dress?"

Lottie brightened. "Oh, yes…"

They talked of lace, muslin and silk then Lottie took her leave and Amelia was left to wonder yet again when she would get to plan her own wedding. A few minutes later she heard footsteps on the stairs and glanced out into the corridor to see her mother returning from a luncheon engagement.

On impulse she said, "Mama, may I speak to you for a moment?"

"Yes, dear. You can talk to me while I change for dinner."

Amelia followed her mother into her bedroom and sat down on a chair to one side of the bed as Mrs Daventry's maid, McInnes, helped her out of the lovely green and yellow walking outfit and into an elegant grey evening dress. The colour was too pale to suit Amelia, who mused that she would wear brightly coloured evening dresses when she was married. And emeralds or possibly rubies.

"What did you wish to discuss?" her mother prompted.

Amelia pulled her thoughts back to the present. "Lottie said something that seemed strange to me but perhaps I am failing to comprehend the matter fully. She said Mrs Saverney wanted the wedding to take place as soon as possible, maybe next month."

Mrs Daventry frowned as McInnes buttoned up the side of the evening dress. "It does seem a little odd."

"It is Lottie's family who will gain financially from the wedding, not Mrs Saverney's."

"Perhaps she simply wishes to see Mr Saverney settled as soon as possible for his own happiness. When did she talk of the wedding with Charlotte?"

"Mr Saverney conveyed the information while he and Lottie were riding in the park."

"Then that explains the matter." Mrs Daventry sat down in front of her dressing table so that McInnes could dress her hair. "Doubtless, it is he who is impatient to be married and he used his mother as an excuse to suggest it."

"Oh, I see." It still seemed peculiar to Amelia but, since she knew little of men's behaviour, she accepted her mother's explanation and forgot about the matter.

CHAPTER THREE

LOTTIE AWOKE and, as always these last few weeks, her first conscious thought was of her fiancé, Mr Saverney. She gave a laugh of delight. She had never known such love was possible and had no idea what she had done to deserve it, but suddenly her life was a paradise. If she could devote the rest of her life to being with Mr Saverney and making him happy then she could not imagine being unhappy ever again.

She hoped Amelia would find someone to love soon, as she knew her friend had been feeling left out recently. They had known each other from infancy, both the same age and of old landed families, so their friendship was encouraged. In all honesty, there had been times when she envied Amelia's beauty and ability to charm everyone around her and Lottie had secretly feared that no one would ever look beyond Amelia and see her, but that had been before Mr Saverney.

Lottie was one of the few people who really knew Amelia and, underneath her love of balls and pretty things, was intelligence, wit and a good heart. It was Amelia who had enabled Lottie to take the occasional risk or speak her mind and Lottie knew she would have been greatly the poorer without Amelia's friendship. So now she wanted Amelia to have her own share of joy - there must be someone as wonderful as Mr Saverney waiting for her.

Her thoughts drifted to wedding preparations and she was thinking about flowers for the church when an exclamation of horror interrupted her thoughts and she jolted back to reality. She could now hear her parents' voices, loud and agitated. It was unusual for them to argue and, from the tone of her mother's voice, she was distressed over something.

Lottie hastily got out of bed, put a wrap on over her nightgown and hurried into the corridor. She paused for a moment, hesitant to interrupt, but the voices continued, quiet, as if they did not want to be overheard, but alarmed. She got up her courage and knocked on the door to her mother's bedroom. She opened it to see her parents standing, her father fully dressed while her mother was still in her nightgown.

Mama was a strong-willed woman who had always looked with contempt upon women who fainted or developed nervous complaints. Now, though, she was pallid and looked on the verge of collapse and the sight of her like this scared Lottie.

"What is wrong?" she asked from the doorway and when her parents turned their gazes to her their expressions grew even more distraught.

* * *

Amelia was startled to be led into the drawing room when she arrived at Lottie's house, instead of simply going to her bedroom or garden as she usually did. The room was large and elegant, even though it was not decorated in the latest style and even though some unworthy person might have said that it was a little shabby. Neither her family nor Lottie's had much money so neither of their rented houses were in the most fashionable squares in Edinburgh's New Town, nor were their furnishings grand, but if both of them were to marry well – as Lottie was set to do – they could greatly improve the family fortunes.

"I'll check if Miss Harrington is up to any visitors, Miss Daventry," the maid said and vanished before Amelia could question these unsettling words. She took a seat on an elaborately carved but uncomfortable chair.

After a sufficiently long wait that Amelia was nearly beside herself with curiosity and worry, the maid returned. "I'm very sorry, Miss, but neither Miss Harrington nor Mrs Harrington can see you right now. Miss Harrington asked if you'd be good enough to return this afternoon."

"But what has occurred?" Amelia asked, shocked. Charlotte had only refused to see her once before and that was when she had been ill.

The maid looked uncomfortable. "I cannot speak of it, Miss."

"What about Mr Benjamin Harrington or Mr Harrington? Are they available?"

"They're not at home, Miss Daventry. I'm truly sorry."

She looked close to tears so Amelia hastened to say, "It is not your fault. Just let Miss Harrington know that I will return later as she requests."

"Yes, Miss."

Amelia left that house feeling disturbed and mystified. Had there been a death in the family? Was someone ill? Had Amelia herself done something to mortally offend her friend? By luncheon Amelia's head was full of questions but no answers.

She was frowning over a glass of lemonade when her mother rushed into the dining room, still wearing her walking clothes. "I have heard the most dreadful rumour," Mrs Daventry said, removing her hat, "but it cannot be true. You saw Charlotte Harrington this morning, did you not?"

Amelia denied this, her worry escalating as she

explained what had happened.

Her mother sat down heavily on the dining chair opposite. "Then it is true."

"What is?" Amelia begged. "Please tell me at once what has happened."

* * *

Lottie heard of Amelia's return with dread, fearing she would burst into yet more tears and be unable to explain a thing. She steeled herself and carefully walked down the stairs on shaking legs. Amelia left the drawing room and met her at the foot of the stairs, clasping her hand. For some reason Lottie was aware of how dull she must look with her plain features and in her unadorned white morning dress next to Amelia's beauty and style. They walked back into the drawing room, which was lit only by candles, the curtains closed to protect the furniture and tapestries from fading. They sat down, Amelia pulling her chair close to Lottie's.

"Mr Saverney cannot have done something so despicable?" Amelia burst out.

She wondered who had told her. Surely there could not be gossip already? If only she could say it was not true. "He... Mr Saverney ... Yes, he has left me..."

"Eloped with some unspeakable woman?"

Lottie dug her fingernails into her palms. "I know nothing against her character, just that she is working class."

"She was a maid in his own house?"

"Yes."

"How did he inform you? Did he send you a letter?"

Lottie shook her head, the reminder causing a stab of pain.

"Nothing?" Amelia's voice shook with fury. "He left you to discover his actions with no word or warning whatsoever?"

Lottie nodded, unable to speak, head bent over as she tried to blink back more tears. She had never thought Mr Saverney was capable of doing anything callous; she still wanted to believe that it was all a mistake and he would appear at any moment to explain the misunderstanding, but she was beginning to accept that he truly had left her and the pain of it was worse than anything she had ever known before.

Amelia rang for a maid and left the room to speak to her. Lottie heard her asking for tea to be brought in to them. As the door opened again Lottie hastily wiped her eyes and told herself she was fine; she would find a way to get through this.

Amelia resumed her seat and took Lottie's hand and her sympathy nearly made Lottie fall apart. "He is clearly the worst form of cad and was never in any way worthy of you."

The words, clearly supposed to reassure her, only made her feel more miserable. She had thought she knew everything about Mr Saverney and how could she ever trust her instincts about people again if he had deceived her? "I loved him."

"I know." Amelia squeezed her hand. "But I do not believe he was ever the man he pretended to be."

"Do you think he ever loved me?"

"I do not know."

Neither did she and somehow that was the worst part.

CHAPTER FOUR

SAVERNEY'S SHAMEFUL behaviour and desertion of Lottie were on the lips of everyone by the next day. Her parents were discussing the matter over breakfast. Half the guests were making cruel jokes about it at a picnic she attended; indeed she left early or she would have rebuked them in a way her mother would have been displeased about. Then her father came home mid-afternoon and said the matter had been the sole source of conversation at his club. Amelia grew increasingly worried. How was Lottie ever to get over this if it was such a source of gossip?

She paid a visit to her friend that afternoon and found Lottie shut in her room, sitting by the window, pretending to read, but her pale face and red-rimmed eyes spoke their own tale. Amelia pulled a chair close to her friend's and removed her gloves and hat, automatically touching her hair to make sure it had not become disordered.

"How was the picnic?" Lottie asked and it clearly took an effort for her to feign interest.

"Quite dull. You certainly missed nothing exciting."

Lottie aimed a shrewd look at her. "Are people gossiping over me?"

"They are talking about what a revolting specimen

Saverney is. You, naturally, have everyone's sympathy."

Lottie looked dubious about this. She was innocent but not naïve.

"Perhaps you would feel better for a little fresh air. We could stroll round the park or visit the shops?"

Lottie shook her head. "Mama says the same thing but I just cannot face them all yet."

"You will feel better soon." Amelia wondered which of them she was trying to convince. She had never seen Lottie in so broken a state and had no idea what to do to help her. Worse, she remembered her selfish dislike of the engagement and realised what a terrible friend she had been. She would refuse offers of marriage for an entire year if only she could see Lottie happy again.

They spoke for a while longer but Lottie seemed too tired and distracted to cope with much conversation. When Amelia went downstairs she saw Mr Benjamin Harrington looking out of the library window, a shuttered expression on his normally expressive face, and walked into the room to join him.

"I have never seen her so dejected," she confessed.

"Nor I. I could kill Saverney for this," Mr Harrington said.

"Yes. Do you think poison would be a sufficiently unpleasant death for him?"

He gave a wan smile and said, "It is worth considering."

* * *

Mr Brightford, too, was worried for Mr Harrington's family. He had spent the morning looking over horses to find a good quality matching pair for his new curricle, with several friends, and aside from the quality of the aforementioned geldings, Saverney's desertion of Miss Harrington was all anyone wanted to talk about.

When Brightford had first heard of the scandal he had been appalled. He had always thought Saverney to be a wishy-washy fellow, following the instructions of his mother like a child, but he never expected him to rebel in such a cruel, destructive manner. Saverney had ruined his own standing in society and left Miss Harrington the subject of damaging gossip that might haunt her for the rest of her life.

Miss Harrington was a young lady who had Brightford's greatest respect, her demure behaviour, modesty and quiet warmth impressing him. She was the opposite of that irritating friend of hers. Miss Daventry might be a beauty of the first order but she was all too aware of the fact and her arrogance, mercenary pursuit of a wealthy husband and outspoken tongue annoyed him every time he saw her.

Miss Harrington was faultless in this matter and she must be suffering badly from Saverney's treatment and from being the focus of everyone's interest in the worst way. Without the support of people around her, this event could ruin her life. Brightford resolved to visit her brother the next day and express his desire to help the family in any way he could. He doubted the self-centred Miss Daventry was even concerned about her friend...

* * *

At something of a loss without Lottie beside her, Amelia put on her riding clothes and took her mare for a ride in the park, accompanied by one of the grooms. A couple of men, barely older than her, paid her compliments but she was not interested in silly flattery. She tried to think of some little gift she could get for her friend but such things seemed meaningless compared to the enormity of Lottie's pain. It seemed like a terrible failure on her own part that she could do nothing to help.

Worse still was the memory of her jealousy of Lottie's engagement. She was not used to finding fault with herself but could not deny the conviction that Lottie had always been a far better friend than she herself had.

Lottie's engagement to a wealthy man had been a matter of great importance to her family. They had used to have a good deal of money but Lottie's grandfather had been an idle second son who inherited the estate when his sibling died then spent the rest of his life gambling money away and doing no work to keep the estate in order. It was Lottie's father who had struggled to re-build the estate, in the end only saving it - Lottie had revealed - by marrying her mother. The story was an interesting one, unlike that of Amelia's own family who had apparently never been very wealthy. As a child, Amelia had asked Mr Harrington if she could adopt his family's thrilling story for her own. He had looked doubtfully at her and expressed relief that his daughter did not have Amelia's imagination.

Lottie was someone who hated being the centre of attention - part of the reason she had always been such an ideal friend for Amelia - and would probably have preferred to return to her family's country estate until the rumours died down, if not longer. However, Amelia knew that Lottie's parents would never allow this, still expecting her to make a good marriage. This made Lottie's situation even more difficult.

Amelia returned home in a depressed mood and half-heartedly worked on a watercolour painting until she had to change for dinner. Walker asked if she felt unwell when Amelia said she did not care what dress she wore; she could muster no enthusiasm for such things.

"How is Charlotte?" her mother asked over the first course.

Amelia looked down at her soup, appetite fleeing as she remembered the ghostlike creature her friend had turned into. "She is devastated. How could he have treated her like that? Why did he ask her to marry him?"

"That might well have been pressure from his mother. Mrs Saverney is a strong-willed woman, keen to have her son married to a girl of good family as soon as possible after the late Mr Saverney's sudden death."

"Nothing could possibly excuse his conduct."

"If he marries this chit then he will be excluded from good society," Mr Daventry said, putting down his spoon and dabbing his mouth with a serviette.

"He should be hanged."

Mr Daventry patted Amelia's shoulder. "He certainly behaved in an unnecessarily cruel manner and I am sure he will suffer for it."

He certainly would if Amelia ever set eyes on him again.

* * *

Benjamin walked to the bar of his club and ordered a double whiskey. He was not usually a heavy drinker but he was so furious over Saverney's treatment of Lottie that he wanted to kill someone. Tonight he needed to relax over a card game or two and drink himself into a better mood.

He joined a card table that was just getting started, preparing for a game of piquet. As he sat down his eyes fell upon the man opposite him and he recognised his former friend and the former object of his affection, Mr Duneton, who glared at him, got to his feet with a scrape of his chair and stalked to another table. Benjamin slugged back the rest of his whiskey and ignored the way the other players went quiet.

After another long minute a new gentleman took Mr Duneton's place and the game began. When he won the first hand he began to relax but then he heard Saverney's name mentioned at the adjacent table. He looked over at the group of young men.

The gaudily dressed, red-faced gentleman talking,

clearly more than a little drunk, was Mr Wenton, someone he knew slightly. "… Clearly thought she had got him under her thumb by forcing him to propose to the Harrington chit, but I had seen his pretty maid and Miss Harrington could not compare…"

Benjamin was not even aware of having got to his feet until he dragged Wenton out of his chair. "You are speaking of my sister, sir, and I demand satisfaction."

Wenton blanched, protesting that he had meant no offence, then several gentlemen from Benjamin's table pulled him off the man and tried to calm him down. He was too angry to remain, though, and stalked out of the club in a worse mood than when he had entered it.

Damn Saverney. When he next saw the man, Benjamin would find a way to make him suffer for what he had done.

CHAPTER FIVE

AMELIA HAD SPENT a pleasant hour on awaking with a book of poetry by Robert Burns. Her mother would have destroyed the book had she known of its existence, even though the poet had recanted some of his more liberal views before his death four years ago. Amelia loved the poetry, though, and the rich Scottish language it was written in, something else that society frowned upon these days. Speaking or writing Scottish dialect or with a Scottish accent was considered uncultured, something Amelia privately thought ludicrous.

She let Walker help her into a simple morning dress, the plain white design improved by lace and embroidery, and, as always, did not correct Walker's use of the word *lassie*.

At breakfast the butler held out a tray for Mrs Daventry upon which was an invitation. Amelia brightened at the sight of it, wondering what form of entertainment it promised. She lowered her cup of chocolate and waited.

"Mr Brightford is holding a ball," Mama said, "and has invited us."

"Oh, no." Amelia groaned, her hopes shattered. "If he holds a ball it will be as tedious as he is."

Mr Daventry put his newspaper down on the dining table. "I do not know what you have against Mr Brightford. He is intelligent and not unkind."

Amelia laughed. "Yet the best you can say of him is that he is *not unkind*. He is sneering and condescending and I am quite sure he dislikes me as heartily as I dislike him."

"Then you do not wish to attend the ball?" Mama queried.

Amelia paused with her cup halfway to her mouth, considering the astonishing idea of turning down such an invitation. Even a ball held by Mr Brightford was better than none. "I suppose I could suffer his company for one evening."

She finished her breakfast then took the carriage to see Lottie and discuss the important subject of ball gowns. It was not generally permissible to call upon an acquaintance before one in the afternoon, a morning call actually occurring any time in the afternoon before dinner, but she and Lottie had long-since done away with such formalities, both usually dressed and breakfasted by the unfashionably early time of ten o'clock.

"I do not know if it is a good idea," Lottie said, as they sat in her bedroom, when Amelia mentioned the subject of the ball. Her family had, of course, received invitations too but, even though three weeks had past since Mr Saverney's desertion, Lottie had attended no social events. It had been as much as Amelia could do to coax her to the park or to the shops.

"Nonsense," Amelia said firmly, an image in her mind of Lottie becoming a permanent recluse. "Nothing could be better. Everyone will be agog to meet Mr Brightford's cousins and find out if his odiousness runs in the family…"

"That is unkind," Lottie objected but Amelia saw her smile.

"… So no one will even think about any other gossip. Besides, Mr Saverney is old news now. This is your chance to have some fun and you are taking it."

"It would be pleasant to dance again and forget about … the past. Not that anyone is likely to ask me to dance."

"I wager you are entirely wrong there and to prove your side of the bet you will have to attend the ball."

Lottie smiled. "Very well."

Amelia gave an internal sigh of relief at this victory and got back to the subject of what they should both wear.

✳ ✳ ✳

Amelia entered the assembly room with her parents where Mr Brightford was greeting guests, two unknown men at his side. He introduced the brown-haired man, who looked to be a few years older than him, as Mr Alexander Fenbridge. The blond man, who seemed in his mid-twenties like Brightford, was another cousin, Mr Nathaniel Fenbridge. They bowed and smiled at Amelia and her parents in a way that suggested a friendliness of character she instantly liked.

Another group entered the room so they could not linger to talk to the men, but two good-looking new gentlemen were an excellent start to the evening. She curtsied and exchanged greetings with several acquaintances, the ball already more than half full of people in full dress, the pale colours of the unmarried women's dresses competing with the brighter ones of the married women and many of the men's outfits were equally grand. Amelia paused to admire a blue gauze gown covered in pink satin roses, ignoring her mother's comment that several women had gowns with an indecently low décolletage.

Across the noisy room Amelia saw Lottie, Benjamin and their parents arrive so she hurried over and pulled her friend to one side to ask what she thought of Mr Brightford's cousins.

"They seem most pleasant," Lottie said. She was looking about her with a nervous frown, jittery as if waiting for someone to make a comment about Mr Saverney.

"They seem most handsome," Amelia corrected, getting her attention. "Do you know if they are married?"

"No."

"Then we must find out. Let us approach Mrs Fraser. As Mr Brightford's sister, she will know everything we could possibly wish to discover."

Mrs Fraser, a friendly woman quite the opposite in character from her brother, was most helpful. Neither gentleman was married and she described them both as having excellent characters. She was just getting onto the important subject of wealth when another guest unfortunately drew her away.

Both ladies were then asked to dance, after which they - standing with Lottie's parents and brother - ran into the gentlemen themselves. The men fetched drinks for them and Mr Nathaniel Fenbridge declared what a wonderful evening he was having, his easy good humour causing smiles all round.

"I know that you are cousins of Mr Brightford but are you cousins to each other, sir, or brothers?" Amelia asked.

"Brothers," Mr Nathaniel Fenbridge said. "Alex here is the wealthy one while I am a useless younger sibling." He smiled and Amelia caught Benjamin's melting expression. *Oh, no: not again!* she thought. Still, the man was attractive with golden hair and piercingly blue eyes - she could not fault Benjamin's taste. It was a shame he was not the one with the money. Not that Mr Alexander Fenbridge was unattractive in the least, just as tall and broad-shouldered as his brother but with light brown hair.

"Not useless at all," Mr Alexander Fenbridge was answering. "My brother is an excellent estate manager, far better than me. I rely on him a great deal and there is plenty of land for us to share."

"And do you spend much time in London?" Amelia asked.

"We visit the capital quite often," Mr Nathaniel Fenbridge replied. When Amelia asked what it was like he said, "It is an exciting place full of exhibitions and interesting places to visit along with constant invitations to dinners and balls. Indeed, sometimes there are not enough hours in the day to fit everything in."

Amelia daydreamed over this, almost able to imagine herself there.

"Still," he concluded, "I prefer the countryside. I greatly enjoy the everyday concerns of running an estate."

"We are in agreement on that," Benjamin said at once, without doubt smitten. "I always feel more useful at the estate, which is a, er, pleasant feeling." He tailed off, going red.

"Indeed."

They discussed estate matters for several rather dull minutes then, during a pause, Mr Alexander Fenbridge asked Lottie to dance. She agreed, cheeks slightly flushed, and Amelia was delighted at how well the evening was succeeding in bringing her out of her depression.

"May I request a dance with you, Miss Daventry?" Mr Nathaniel Fenbridge asked and Amelia willingly assented. Before they moved away he expressed a hope for further discussions with Benjamin, ensuring that gentleman's happiness for the rest of the evening.

The quadrille was a lively dance and Mr Nathaniel Fenbridge an excellent dancer so Amelia lost herself for a time in the elaborate moves. When the dance finally came to a close they rejoined the group and even Mr Brightford's arrival could not dampen Amelia's enjoyment.

"I must congratulate you on an excellent ball, Mr Brightford," she said with no sarcasm at all.

"Miss Daventry," he said in a mocking tone, "I am pleasantly surprised that you find it so."

"I am pleasantly surprised myself," she responded in a

tone that said she was in fact astonished that he had succeeded so well.

"Miss Daventry…"

She turned with a smile which froze at the sight of the Duke of Elborough.

"… May I have this dance?"

She sought for a reason to refuse him and could think of nothing. "Certainly, Your Grace."

He was a good dancer, but he stood too close to her and she did not like the way he looked at her, as if she were a snack he wished to devour. However, her spirits rose at the sight of Lottie dancing with Mr Brightford and she could almost like him for this kindness. The music, which she would normally have enjoyed, went on for far too long. When it ended she smiled politely to the Duke and, for fear that he would attempt to strike up an uncomfortable conversation, begged him to fetch her a drink. As he did so she returned to the group where Mr Nathaniel Fenbridge and Benjamin were having an animated discussion about horses. Lottie and Mr Brightford walked back then he was called away by another guest.

Lottie leaned forward to speak to her but was prevented by the Duke's reappearance with drinks which he presented to the two ladies with a smile. He then hovered at Amelia's side, making small talk. She finished her drink and, thankfully, Mr Alexander Fenbridge asked her to dance, after which time the Duke had vanished.

The evening was drawing to a close when she caught sight of Mr Brightford talking to a dark haired gentleman she did not know. The gentleman caught her glance and his eyes widened in clear admiration. He said something to Mr Brightford, with a nod in Amelia's direction. She looked away, hiding a smile, and tried to look surprised when the men approached her.

"Miss Daventry," Mr Brightford said, "may I introduce Mr Wrackley, a friend of my cousins who accompanied them on their visit here. Wrackley, this is Miss Daventry."

He bowed and gave her a warm smile that seemed to reach deep inside her. She curtsied, heart beating loudly in her chest. He was the most handsome man she had ever seen, tall and strong-looking with warm brown eyes that caused a strange nervousness in her.

"It is a great pleasure, Miss Daventry. May I request a dance?"

They both glanced over at the musicians, who were packing away their instruments.

"Unfortunately I cannot accept your offer," she said.

"I regret exceedingly that we did not meet earlier tonight," he said, "but I will be staying with Brightford for a while so I hope to see you again soon."

Amelia saw Brightford roll his eyes at this but she was charmed by the man. "I am sure you shall. That is, Mr Brightford and I tend to be invited to the same events, although I am not convinced that he takes any pleasure in them."

"I am not much of a dancer," Brightford said, not denying her words.

"I am astonished that anyone could object to any event that included such charming company. Miss Daventry, would it be overly forward to request a dance with you at the next ball we both attend?"

"I would be happy to save one for you."

"A cotillian?"

"Gladly as that is one of my favourites."

The gentlemen bowed and withdrew then Lottie said farewell and left with her parents and Amelia's own parents announced it was time to return home.

She took her leave of Mr Wrackley and his cousins. In the carriage she thought that Lottie had seemed in far better spirits than she had been since the broken engagement and even Brightford was in a less offensive mood than usual. And Mr Wrackley… Amelia was almost afraid to think about him for fear she had just dreamed such a man. She would be sensible about the matter and see how things went at their next meeting. She instinctively smiled at the thought of seeing him again. Yes, she thought, the evening had been a great success.

CHAPTER SIX

DESPITE THE BALL having lasted until the early hours of the morning, Lottie awoke at her usual time and put on a plain morning dress, utterly different from the lacy muslin gown she had worn the night before. It had been the pleasantest of evenings and her fears of people referring to her broken engagement had proved unfounded. Perhaps Amelia had been correct and Lottie had been hiding away unnecessarily. The sun was shining outside and it would be nice to go to the park or visit a few haberdashers and perfumers with Amelia.

She walked into the dining room, the smell of food after the previous night's exertions giving her a keen appetite. Then her parents turned to look at her with unhappy expressions she had come to dread and, with a knotting sensation in her stomach, she knew somehow that the cause was the same as on the last occasion.

"Is it Mr Saverney?"

Her mother walked over to put an arm round her shoulder, an affectionate gesture that was entirely out of character. Lottie felt sick as her mother said, "That man has had the effrontery to return to Edinburgh with …"

"His bride?"

"If that word can be applied to such a low creature."

"I see. Thank you."

She turned and walked out of the room, up the long flight of stairs and into the bedroom. The dark oak panelling on the walls made them close in around her until she could barely breathe and she felt like a prisoner. The humiliations would never be over; she would have to endure this for the rest of her life. Lottie, who was known for her demure placid character, picked up a bottle of perfume and flung it with all her strength at the wall opposite. It shattered, leaving behind jagged fragments of glass and an overpowering flowery smell.

Lottie looked in horror at what she had done and sank to the floor, a hand over her mouth so the servants would not hear her sobs.

* * *

Amelia lay in bed thinking of the ball the previous night and of meeting Mr Wrackley. Just remembering the warm expression in his eyes made her want to dance round the room. Surely this was it? This was what love felt like?

She had never thought much about the subject before. Her own parents had had an arranged marriage and while they clearly had a fondness and respect for each other, she did not believe they had ever been in love. She had expected such a practical arrangement to suit her but now it seemed inadequate, sad, even. Would it not be wonderful to spend a lifetime with someone who could make her feel so happy?

She frowned then as she thought of Lottie, understanding for the first time some part of what Lottie had felt she had with Saverney. To feel like this then lose the man she loved - it must have been almost unbearable. And Lottie was the very last person to deserve to be treated that way. She was recovering, though. She had been far more like her old self last night, dancing and smiling.

The attention of Mr Brightford's cousins to Lottie had been particularly good for her and Amelia thought with gratitude and liking of the men. This thought led back to Mr Wrackley and she wondered when she would see him again. Perhaps in a few days. Perhaps today.

She jumped out of bed and ran across the room to her wardrobe.

By the time Walker arrived with her breakfast, Amelia had scattered half her clothes around the room.

"Walker, which dress makes me look the prettiest? No, not just pretty but beautiful?"

* * *

Benjamin had left the house early for a ride in the park and, having been waylaid by an old acquaintance, had missed the hour when the family sat down to breakfast. It was not obligatory, he told himself as he handed Caesar over to the head groom, pausing briefly to stroke the horse's soft nose.

The house was ominously silent when he entered it but he paid no heed, still in a euphoric mood after meeting Mr Nathaniel Fenbridge last night. He knew he should be cautious, that his tendres had caused nothing but trouble so far, but just the thought of seeing him and talking to him again made Benjamin happy. He ate a solitary breakfast then ran upstairs to check on his sister. She had been brighter the last few days and had been in excellent spirits after last night's ball. Since he had no particular plans for the day he thought she might wish him to act as her escort on a trip to some of the local shops. The city was changing constantly at the moment with the various additions to the New Town, of which their own house was a part. He understood that a new milliners shop had opened that might interest Lottie.

He knocked on his sister's door and, since it was ajar, pushed it open. Lottie turned in her seat at the dressing table. One look at her face brought all his concerns back again. "What has happened?"

In a voice bleached of emotion, she said, "Mr Saverney has returned to Edinburgh with his new wife."

For a moment he refused to believe his own ears. "Damn the man."

Lottie rubbed her face with her hands, expression so defeated that it hurt him to see. The gossip had begun to lessen. I tried to be brave…"

"… You have been very brave, my dear. I know our parents have been proud of how well you handled the situation."

"But now I am back at the starting point. The gossip will begin again worse than ever and every time I leave the house I will also face the fear of seeing him again and experiencing even worse pain and humiliation." Tears ran down her pale cheeks. "I do not know if I can go through it all again. Oh, why could he not have stayed away?"

He sat with her as she cried but had rarely felt so useless. She refused to leave her room, pleading a headache, but insisted he continue with his day, saying she would be better later. It was a claim he doubted. He did not know how to contain his fury but then he realised, with savage pleasure, that he did not need to. As he strode out of the house he knew exactly where to vent his anger.

* * *

Amelia's family carriage came to a halt and she got out to wait for her mother. They were going to look at fabrics for making into a couple of new outfits for Amelia. While it was always highly pleasing to have new clothes, the reminder that the season during which she had expected to be married was halfway over was a disturbing one.

Her gaze lifted instinctively to Edinburgh Castle high above, admiring its elegance and splendour. What must it be like to live in such a place, to have the best clothes, the best of everything, more wealth than could be spent in a lifetime, being envied by everyone..?

She started when a masculine voice spoke her name. Unused to being so addressed in public by gentlemen, she looked around, ready to put the man in his place, then her breath caught at the sight of Mr Wrackley. He and Mr Brightford - whom she belatedly also noticed - bowed to her and she curtsied, noting as she did so that Mr Wrackley looked even more dashing in the daylight. His boots and buckskin breeches clung to his legs in a manner she felt almost too embarrassed to observe; just visible beneath his dark tailcoat were his shirt and waistcoat while his neckcloth was tied in an elaborate fashionable knot. He carried his hat and gloves in one hand while the other rested on his watch fob. His dark hair and eyes were all the more striking in the sunshine and his high cheekbones and full lips convinced her he must be the most handsome man in the country.

She wished her own walking dress was more brightly coloured, but as she was an unmarried woman it was plain cream. At least the embroidery on her shawl and the ribbons on her straw hat were a bright blue which matched her eyes. That must surely look fairly pleasing?

"How delightful to see you again so soon, Miss Daventry," Mr Wrackley said, with an admiring expression. We are just meeting Mr Brightford's cousins for luncheon."

"We are in fact due now," Mr Brightford pointed out with his usual lack of charm and manners.

Amelia ignored him but could not fail to respond to her mother's shockingly badly timed arrival when the men turned to bow to her.

"We keep meeting just to immediately part," Amelia

said to Mr Wrackley. "I hope our next encounter will allow us a longer conversation."

"And a dance," he agreed, smiling. "You promised me a cotillian."

He had remembered their exact conversation, she noted, delighted. "I have not forgotten."

He and Mr Brightford left and she turned at once to her mother: "Is my hat on straight? Do I look well?"

"You look lovely," Mrs Daventry reassured her with an amused expression.

"I should have asked which balls he would be attending."

"That would have been forward." Her mother got into the carriage and Amelia followed her. "In any case, as a friend of Mr Brightford, Mr Wrackley will no doubt attend many of the same events as us."

"Yes," Amelia breathed, thinking: *how wonderful.*

* * *

Benjamin pounded on the door and, when it opened, pushed past the elderly butler, saying, "Where is that rat Saverney?"

The man gave an instinctive glance at one of the internal doors. "Sir, you cannot…"

Benjamin strode to the door and flung it open. Saverney was seated inside with two women whom Benjamin ignored. Saverney jumped up in a nervous manner. "Harrington…"

"It does not surprise me, sir, that you have the nerve and cruelty to return here, but I am surprised you have the stupidity to do so." He pulled off a glove and flung it at Saverney's feet. "I demand satisfaction for your despicable behaviour."

The women - Saverney's mother and also, presumably, his bride - had risen and protested this in alarmed voices.

Once again he ignored them, focused solely on the man in front of him. "Will you accept my challenge or cry off and prove yourself an utter coward in front of your family?"

"Surely we can discuss the matter?" Saverney said, eyes darting to the glove then back to Benjamin's face.

"It is far too late for that. You have behaved like the worst kind of scoundrel to my sister. Accept my challenge or leave Edinburgh immediately, publicly branded a coward."

Saverney bent down and picked up the glove, his reluctance showing in every movement.

Benjamin nodded in satisfaction then turned and stalked out.

CHAPTER SEVEN

MR BRIGHTFORD frowned at the letter, mind reeling. It was a rash move but he could not blame Harrington.

"Is everything all right, Jolly?" Alex asked, he, Nathan and Wrackley pausing in their breakfasts to look at him.

"I have just received a letter from Mr Benjamin Harrington asking me to be his second in a duel." He explained what had occurred with Mr Saverney and that the man had now re-emerged.

"Poor Miss Harrington," Alex said, frowning. "To have to worry about her brother on top of such a distressing situation."

"It is Mr Harrington I am concerned about," Nathan exclaimed. "He could die. Jolly, is he a good shot? Is Saverney?"

Brightford considered this. Duels were not common these days but he did not believe Harrington would falter. "I have never seen Mr Saverney shoot but Harrington has a good eye."

"You must give him some pointers," Nathan said. "You are the best shot I know. I suppose he cannot be dissuaded from this course of action? An apology to the family by Mr Saverney?"

"Saverney's very presence inflames the situation, particularly with his new bride in tow. An apology six weeks ago might have been good enough but I doubt it would do any good now. Harrington is a good fellow, but hot-tempered. He will not change his mind. Indeed, had my sister ever been treated in such a manner I would have reacted in just the same way."

"You should go to see him immediately," Nathan insisted and, in spite of the seriousness of the situation, Brightford could not help an inward smile. Harrington had certainly made a favourable impression on his cousin.

* * *

Lottie grabbed Amelia's hands, eyes wide with alarm. "You will never believe it. Benjy has challenged Mr Saverney to a duel."

"Excellent." Amelia exclaimed, proud and not in the least surprised at Mr Harrington's action. At least someone was finally doing something to put that hateful man in his place.

Lottie dropped her hands and looked at her with an expression of anger Amelia had never seen before on her face. "How can you say such a thing? Benjy could die."

"Nonsense," Amelia retorted. "Mr Saverney is already entirely in the wrong. He would be a fool to make his situation any worse by harming Benjamin."

"He will hardly be thinking so rationally. They will both have guns. Anything could happen."

She paced up and down until Amelia caught her arm and led her to a chair, she herself sitting on the bed opposite her friend, a small part of her mind wondering why the room smelt quite so strongly of perfume.

"I am sure your brother will be fine…"

"If only he would see reason and cancel the duel. I begged him."

"Lottie, he is doing this to avenge the wrong Mr Saverney has done to you, because he loves you. If I were a man it is exactly what I would do…."

Lottie managed a smile at this.

"… And I sincerely hope that Mr Saverney suffers an extremely unpleasant injury."

Lottie hesitated then said, "Nothing fatal."

"No, no. Merely an arm or leg or shoulder injury. Their seconds will ensure nothing more serious occurs. Who has Benjamin chosen as his second?"

"Mr Brightford."

"There then. Mr Brightford is far too dull to allow matters get out of hand."

Lottie gave a short laugh. "You are unfair to the poor man. Yet you are right, also: he is dependable enough that I believe I can rely on him to keep Benjy safe."

"Of course."

"Perhaps I should write him a letter imploring him to do so?"

"Certainly, although that might be a little improper so I would not mention it to your parents if I were you."

Lottie looked beseechingly at Amelia. "You truly believe it will be all right?"

"I do and, indeed, when Benjamin returns safely I hope you will tell him that you are proud of him."

"I will do no such thing or he might take the notion of regularly fighting duels."

Amelia fought back a smile with only moderate success. "I do not think he would run quite so wild as that."

* * *

Benjamin's valet woke him before dawn. Despite only having had a few hours of sleep, he immediately jumped out of bed to wash and dress, feeling only pleasant anticipation at what lay ahead. For weeks he had had to see

Lottie's misery and at last he could do something about it. He did not intend to kill Saverney, much as the man deserved it, as Saverney did have a family who might actually miss him, besides which Benjamin had no desire to become a fugitive. However, as Amelia had commented to him on her way out of the house yesterday, causing Saverney an embarrassing injury would be a most pleasant thing.

Mr Brightford, along with making all the arrangements for today, had given him a few pointers for the duel. He had also made a half-hearted attempt to talk Benjamin out of the duel then mentioned that his cousin, Mr Nathaniel Fenbridge, was particularly concerned for Benjamin's safety. The latter news was especially welcome as was the idea that he might appear in a remotely heroic light to that gentleman for defending his sister's honour.

He ate a large breakfast and Mr Brightford arrived just as he was finishing. They stepped outside to the sight of a sky striped orange and red then took a carriage to the appointed place which was an area of countryside with no houses in sight. Mr Saverney had not yet arrived so they remained in the carriage to wait.

"Are you nervous?" Mr Brightford asked him.

"Not at all. I have been inactive too long in this."

Mr Brightford nodded his understanding. "It might be tempting to want the man dead for his actions, but that would only make things difficult for you and worse for your family."

"You need not explain; I am not such a fool that I am not aware of that. Besides, every member of my family plus Miss Daventry have already said as much, although Miss Daventry did at least suggest I inflict a painful injury."

Mr Brightford gave a snort of amusement then glanced out of the window. "I think this is them."

Mr Saverney's carriage pulled up next to theirs and he got out accompanied by Sir Bridton, the son of a successful merchant. As Benjamin stepped outside into the unexpectedly cold drizzle of early morning, he saw that Mr Saverney was pale but that his mouth was set in a determined line. He bore little resemblance to the charming liar who had won Lottie's heart.

The gentlemen approached each other and Sir Bridton said, "It is my duty to ascertain whether there is some peaceful way to resolve this argument."

"There is not," Benjamin said flatly.

Sir Bridton opened a box containing two pistols and presented them to first Benjamin then Mr Saverney, who each took one, Benjamin testing its weight and the unfamiliar feel of it.

They took their places back to back - almost like a dance, Benjamin thought - then Sir Bridton gave the word and they began walking. The twenty paces stretched out ahead of him, straining Benjamin's patience. He finally reached twenty and turned round to see Saverney aiming at him. A shot rang out - loud in the stillness - and Benjamin was jerked backwards several steps, arm exploding in pain. Damn, it was his shooting arm too.

He gritted his teeth and lifted his throbbing arm to take aim. Saverney went pale and it was clear how much effort it took for him to remain in place. Benjamin made the shot then he let his arm drop to his side with a groan of pain. The wound was bleeding profusely.

The next thing he knew Brightford was by his side wrapping a neckerchief tightly round his arm, which stopped the bleeding but made the pain even worse.

"Did I hit Saverney?"

Brightford hesitated. "I am not certain how severely hurt he was. He was hit around the stomach area."

Benjamin grimaced at this news. "I was aiming for his arm."

"Do not worry about it. Bridton will fetch him a doctor. You need to return home so that I can do the same for you."

* * *

Lottie had had a restless night worrying about the duel and she awoke hearing male voices downstairs. She realised Mr Brightford had arrived and as she was in her nightgown it was too late to go down and wish Benjy luck. As she listened to them leave the house and the carriage drive away, this increasingly felt like a terrible failure on her part.

She got out of bed and began to dress, not bothering to call her maid at such an hour. The least she could do now was be waiting the moment Benjy returned. She heard her parents descending the stairs and joined them for breakfast, although she could not face the thought of food. She sat with them in silence and sipped a cup of chocolate.

The time inched by until finally they heard the sound of the door knocker. They all jumped to their feet, getting to the hallway as the butler opened the door. Benjy and Mr Brightford entered the house and she went cold at the sight of blood all over her brother's shirt and jacket.

She gasped and her mother made a horrified exclamation as Benjy said, "I am fine."

Mr Brightford added, "It is only his arm that is injured - it looks far worse than it is. I have sent my carriage to bring back the doctor."

"We are grateful, sir," Papa said.

Refusing offers of help, Benjy walked up to his room, the rest of them trailing after him. Lottie helped him to remove his jacket and shirt while her mother rang for a maid to fetch warm water so they could bathe the wound. As he sat on his bed Benjy looked far too young to have been injured in such a way.

"How is Saverney?" Papa asked.

"The wound was either in his side or stomach," Mr Brightford answered, brow furrowed. "It could be serious."

"He could die?"

"Perhaps."

"Then Benjamin would be branded a murderer?" Mama said, clasping her husband's arm.

"I am afraid so, but we must hope it does not come to that. When the doctor arrives I will send my footman out to bring back news of Saverney's condition."

"I can send someone." Her father left to arrange this.

Lottie numbly helped clean Benjamin's arm, wiping away blood until the basin of water was red. She felt sick – Benjy had fought the duel because of her. She should have forbidden it. Now he might have to flee the country, even in his wounded state. They might never see him again.

It was all her fault.

* * *

Amelia was confident that nothing could be amiss as she knocked on the door of Mr Harrington's home. She could not imagine any outcome to the duel except complete success for Benjamin. Indeed, the previous evening it had occurred to her that very likely Mr Saverney would be too much of a coward to even show up to fight and would have to skulk out of Edinburgh a laughingstock.

It was, therefore, with surprise that she found herself led into the drawing room while the maid checked if Lottie could see her. Almost at once Lottie came into the room, face so pale and haggard that Amelia's stomach lurched and foreboding filled her.

"Benjamin..?" He could not be dead?

"He is injured - his arm. The doctor says he will shortly

be recovered…"

"Oh, thank goodness!" Amelia sank into a chair.

"… But Mr Saverney's injury is far worse. If he should die Benjy would have to leave all of us and flee the country."

"It will not come to that," Amelia said, needing to reassure herself as much as Lottie.

"If it does I will have ruined our family."

The words were spoken so softly that Amelia almost thought she had misheard. "How could any of this possibly be your fault?"

"He fought the duel for my sake. I could have found a way to stop him…"

"But I convinced you it would be fine," Amelia exclaimed, getting up and crossing the room to her friend. "If it is anyone's fault, it is mine."

"Not at all. You were simply comforting me."

"No, I was not. I honestly believed Benjamin was so clearly in the right that it would all work out. It was stupid and wrong of me."

"It is not your fault," Lottie insisted.

"Then neither is it yours."

"Perhaps. I simply cannot believe that it has come to this."

"Nor I. What is Benjamin's injury?"

"It is towards the top of his arm. The physician took out the bullet and said Benjy was lucky as it had not caused any loss of movement in his hand and fingers."

Amelia was prevented from answering by the sounds of voices in the hall.

"Oh, that might be news about Mr Saverney's condition. I must go and check."

Lottie darted from the room and Amelia paced back and forth, wondering how she could have been so naïve as to assume no harm would come from the duel. After what seemed an interminable time she heard footsteps approaching and Lottie came in, a smile lighting up her face.

"Everything is well. Mr Saverney is not as badly injured as we feared. The injury is in his side not his stomach, which apparently means he will soon be better."

Amelia embraced her. "I never dreamt of a day when news of Mr Saverney's good health could give me pleasure."

CHAPTER EIGHT

THE DUEL HAD not gone according to plan, Mr Brightford mused, as his carriage slowed to a halt, but at least the outcome had been about as good as one could ask for and Harrington would soon be back to full health. Still, he had left his home at a time when most people were getting back after a good evening's entertainment so he would be glad to relax for an hour or two. He descended from his carriage to the welcome sight of his city house and headed inside, barely making it into the hall, before he was metaphorically pounced upon by his guests.

"We expected you back hours ago," Alex said as the three men came into the hall and watched Brightford remove his wet tailcoat and hat and hand them to his butler.

"Something went wrong." Nathan's normally amiable countenance was grave. "Is Mr Harrington ..?"

"Harrington has a minor arm wound which he will quickly recover from," Brightford reassured them. "I waited with him for word of whether or not Saverney would recover from his injury, but he is now on the mend so there is no need for further concern."

"That is excellent news," Alex said, slapping him on the

back.

Nathan and Wrackley echoed these sentiments, Nathan looking as if a burden had been lifted from him at the words. Brightford then recalled that he had not yet eaten breakfast and since it would shortly be time for luncheon, he had better hurry to do so. He asked his butler to see to it then walked into the dining room, his guests wandering after him like ducklings after their mother. They all sat down around the mahogany dining table and Wrackley and Alex began to discuss their plans for the evening.

Nathan picked up a salt cellar from the table, turning it in his hands. "Do you think Mr Harrington will want visitors? I am not well acquainted with him, of course, and perhaps you think it would not be a good idea?"

Brightford kept a straight face with difficulty. "I have a strong intuition that Harrington would be delighted to receive a visit from you."

* * *

"You are very quiet," Mrs Daventry observed as they sat in the drawing room, embroidering, awaiting a call from one of Mama's friends.

Amelia looked up from her half-finished cushion cover with a frown. "The older I get the more I realise that life is not as simple as it ought to be. I keep expecting things to happen in a just manner and they do not."

Her mother's lips twitched. "What brought on this observation?"

Amelia explained about the duel and how she had been so convinced Benjamin would prevail. At least he was recovering and Lottie could relax and stop worrying about him. Amelia could not help but feel that Mr Brightford had handled the duel badly, allowing the situation to get so badly out of control, but Lottie had insisted that he was of great assistance in its aftermath, which was something.

"He behaved in a brave, if foolhardy, manner and thankfully both he and Mr Saverney will recover," Mama said. "It is good, though, that you see the consequences of thoughtless actions. For a woman in particular, good behaviour is vital as even an ill-advised word can come back to haunt her."

That was not what Amelia had meant and she found it vexing that her mother had taken the opportunity to deliver another lecture. It was not her own behaviour she was concerned about but the behaviour of the world where good people did not always succeed in their endeavours and bad ones were not always punished. Now, more than ever, Benjamin's actions seemed brave to her and she wished it was possible for ladies to achieve as much instead of just worrying about their stupid reputations.

* * *

Benjamin had been half-heartedly reading, already feeling caged by the doctor's insistence he remain indoors today, when the butler announced Mr Nathaniel Fenbridge's arrival. Boredom turned to pleasure and he raced downstairs to the drawing room to his guest.

After exchanging greetings, Mr Fenbridge said, "I am happy to see you up and about after your injury."

"Oh, I feel quite the fraud." Benjamin indicated his arm in its white sling. "My family and doctor are fussing over me all for this tiny gash. I have had worse injuries from being given a shave."

It was a small joke but Mr Fenbridge laughed heartily, making him feel like the wittiest of men.

"Is there any more news of Saverney?"

"He is in no danger," Benjamin said. "That is all I care about. The last I heard he was still abed but he can stay there permanently if it prevents him appearing at mutual social events and distressing my sister."

"And how is Miss Harrington?"

Benjamin grimaced. "I think my injury gave her quite a shock. She will be well now, though. I believe Miss Daventry will be calling later and she always cheers Lottie up."

"Does that mean your family will be attending Mrs McLeod's ball tonight?"

"I imagine so. Will you be going?"

Fenbridge nodded and that was Benjamin's decision on the matter made. They sat drinking tea and discussed the running of an estate for a while then somehow moved onto the subject of criminals, with Benjamin promising to show Mr Fenbridge the place where the infamous masked thief William Brodie had been hanged twelve years previously.

"We saw one poor fellow at the crossroads on the way into Edinburgh, dead and in irons. I dislike seeing even criminals treated in such a way." His compassion made him even more appealing; Benjamin had yet to discover anything that he did not admire about Mr Fenbridge and this feeling was dangerous.

"They are normally used in anatomy class at the College. I am not sure if that is a better fate, although at least it serves to improve our physicians."

"The College?"

"Edinburgh University," Benjamin said. "The city's crowning glory."

"I have heard that it has students from all over the world."

"That is true, not that learning is as popular as it used to be, when all our best thinkers are accused of sedition and sent off to Australia. But I should not criticise or I might be accused myself."

"I swear never to denounce you," Mr Fenbridge said and smiled as if they were sharing a secret. "But, if you are right, at least you could be sure of good company in

Australia."

Benjamin laughed and agreed, but privately thought that no company could be more enjoyable than that of his current companion. He had a feeling he was going to get his heart broken again but the lure was irresistible.

* * *

"What will you wear to the ball tonight?" Amelia asked Lottie as they walked round the nearby park, a line of trees providing some shade from the dazzling sunshine that had followed the earlier rain. The grass smelt fresh and the colours of grass and flowers were richer after being watered.

Lottie nodded to an acquaintance then hesitated, a gloved hand brushing a leaf from her parasol. "I am not sure I will go. The last couple of days have been so tiring…"

"You have to go," Amelia told her, afraid that Lottie could retreat altogether from society given the chance. "Think how Benjamin would feel. He would blame himself."

"But that is nonsense."

"He would think you were so embarrassed over the duel that you refused to attend."

"Then you are right: I must go." Lottie was clearly unhappy over the decision.

"Remember how pleasant Mr Brightford's ball was? You danced nearly every dance and with just about every eligible bachelor in the room." Indeed, Amelia had hopes that Lottie may soon have another suitor.

Lottie smiled. "Hardly that but it was a pleasant evening."

"And there is no reason to think this will be any less so."

"You are right. My mother would say that I am having

a fit of the mopes and must get over it."

Amelia could well imagine it: Mrs Harrington was a stern, autocratic woman. "Is your brother going?"

"Oh, yes. I believe Mr Nathaniel Fenbridge will be there."

Amelia digested the underlying message with interest. That took Mr Fenbridge off the list of eligible men for Lottie but she was pleased for Mr Harrington's sake. As long as it did not end badly. "Do you believe Mr Fenbridge might be someone who could return his feelings?"

"I do not know. It is impossible to judge. They have certainly struck up a strong friendship, though. He came to visit Benjy just this morning and nothing could have aided Benjy's recovery more."

"I am glad. How is Mr Harrington's arm?"

"The doctor says he is entirely satisfied that it is healing properly. Benjy has to wear a sling, which he does not like, but it will not be for long. Have you decided which dress to wear to the ball?"

"Not yet." She would have to look her best: Mr Wrackley would very likely be there.

* * *

This ball was less select than Lady Treeton's had been, the upper classes mixing with wealthy businessmen and the more distinguished academics; the Scottish accents of the middle and working classes mixing with the English accents of the upper class. However, there were handsome men to talk to, pretty dresses to admire and music to dance to so Amelia was content.

She saw Mr Harrington and Mr Nathaniel Fenbridge talking, Benjamin looking so happy and Mr Nathaniel Fenbridge so fond that she had great hopes for them. Lottie, her parents beside her, was talking to Mr

Brightford. Well, that would not do. Mr Brightford would likely never marry anyone and certainly he was far too sharp and bad-tempered for Lottie. She was about to go over and get Lottie away from him when she saw Mr Alexander Fenbridge approach her; a moment later they left together to go to dance. Mr Alexander Fenbridge was a little older than she would have liked for Lottie, perhaps thirty, but this was not an unreasonable age difference. He had been charming so far and had seemed to show a liking for Lottie, although it was difficult to tell as he seemed more reticent than Mr Nathaniel Fenbridge. She remembered how charming Saverney - the rat - had seemed and wished Mr Alexander Fenbridge was not a stranger to the area; the character of a local man would be easier to find out, although again Mr Saverney had deceived everyone.

A voice spoke her name and she recognised it at once and turned to greet Mr Wrackley, trying not to look or sound too eager, or too disinterested. She gave a smile that was hopefully friendly but not excessive. "I am glad to see you again, Mr Wrackley."

"You cannot be as glad as I am."

She had had such flattery fifty times in the past but it had never been anything beyond a pleasant boost to her self-esteem. Now, when Mr Wrackley said any such thing to her she wanted to laugh or throw herself into his arms. This would not do at all. She sternly told herself to be calm. "Are you enjoying your stay in Edinburgh?"

"It is growing more pleasant by the second."

This comment made her feel over-warm and flustered. "And have you visited all the sights?"

"Honestly, I prefer to converse, ride or dance than visit museums or libraries. Does that sound shallow to you?"

"I hope not since I feel much the same way myself."

As the previous music finally came to an end, Mr Wrackley's dark eyes scanned the dance list. "Ah, finally a cotillian. May I request the great honour of this dance with you, Miss Daventry, if you are free?"

She was not but Benjamin would certainly not object to the reprieve. "I would be delighted."

They took their places and the music began. Whenever the dance required him to touch her waist or hand she was acutely aware of the warmth of his hand and of the tingling sensation his touch produced in her body. She had never felt such awareness of another person and their eyes frequently met in gazes that sent pleasurable thrills up and down her spine.

The dance, although some fifteen minutes long with this many couples, was over far too soon and they walked through the crowds away from the dance floor.

She fanned herself, suddenly made light-headed by the extreme heat of the room. Mr Wrackley at once offered his arm and said, "Shall we stand by the doorway to the garden? It might be cooler."

"Yes. Thank you."

It was a little less warm by the open doors. "There are people out on the balcony," Mr Wrackley said. "If you are still warm it would not be improper for us to go outside."

She agreed and, once there, felt a lot better. Mr Wrackley left to fetch her a drink and she stood looking in at the ballroom brightly lit by a vast candelabra and full of talking and dancing guests. No wonder she had felt faint: half of Edinburgh looked to be there. She saw Lottie on Mr Alexander Fenbridge's arm, moving away from the dance area, only to be stopped by Mr Brightford and head back again with him. She smiled, happy that her friend was enjoying the evening.

Her smile faded as she watched the dance begin. Given his attention at this ball and the last one they had attended, Amelia wondered if Mr Brightford could possibly be interested in courting Lottie. It was a thought that alarmed her. Lottie would never be able to cope with his insults and bad temper. No, she told herself, it was far more likely that he actually did possess a speck of goodness and was being kind to Lottie.

She thought that the same was probably, unfortunately, true of Mr Alexander Fenbridge. He seemed to like Lottie but showed no sign of great admiration, let alone love. This meant that the chances of Lottie gaining a husband this season were rapidly diminishing and Amelia was afraid that if Lottie did not get over Saverney's desertion now then she might always feel tainted by it and by the censure of society and never marry.

Mr Wrackley returned with two drinks and she forgot about the presence of anyone else as she thanked him and sipped the lemonade, feeling a strange awareness of his body next to hers. She had never experienced anything like the sensations he aroused in her. It was frightening yet also exciting.

"Would you tell me something of your home?"

He smiled down at her, cheeks dimpling. "What do you wish to know?"

"Something of your life. I do not even know your favourite pastimes or what family you have." It seemed impossible that she actually knew so little when she felt such a strong connection to him.

"I enjoy riding. I have a fondness for cards but I do not gamble excessively. My parents are dead but I have three sisters, two older than me and one younger, along with two younger brothers."

"How pleasant. I think I should have liked siblings, although I do think of Lottie like a sister."

"And your preferred pastimes?"

"I can think of nothing in the world more pleasant than this evening." As soon as the words slipped out she realised it might be improper to suggest his company meant so much to her so soon, but Mr Wrackley looked far from censorious.

His gaze grew more intense, dark gaze as warm as a fire. "I can think of nothing save how beautiful you are."

They gazed at each other and she savoured every

moment and drank in everything about his face.

"There you are, Amelia!"

She jumped at her mother's voice, loud and dry, and just in front of them, in the open doorway.

"I felt a little faint, Mama." She did not know why she should feel guilty. They had not done anything wrong. "Mr Wrackley just brought me outside and fetched me a drink while I recovered."

"If you have done so I think we had better return to the other guests."

They followed her inside, joining Lottie, Benjamin, Mr Brightford, Mr Alexander Fenbridge, Mr Nathaniel Fenbridge and the newly married Mr and Mrs McIvett. The lady was no older than Amelia and the man of no great fortune, but Mrs McIvett was assuming the grandest of airs.

"We had our honeymoon in London, of course. There is nowhere better in the world than our country's great capital."

"I thought we were already in our country's capital," Mr Brightford commented in a slightly bored tone, causing Amelia to feel a momentary warmth towards him.

"Oh, you know what I meant, Mr Brightford," Mrs McIvett simpered, swatting him with her fan. "Do not tease."

Amelia winced at this over-familiarity, particularly with Mr Brightford of all people. He did not respond to the comment but looked even more pained than usual.

Lottie broke the silence by asking what they had liked best about London. She was clearly just being polite and there was nothing hostile in her tone, far from it, but Mrs McIvett looked at her with a cool smile.

"Naturally, my husband's presence at my side gave me the greatest pleasure. Some of us do not scare off our gentlemen."

Lottie froze at the words and, worse, a few of the nearby ladies were cruel enough as to laugh.

Amelia glared at Mrs McIvett. "How fortunate for you that your husband is so easy to please. Come, Charlotte, your mama is looking for you."

She led Lottie away by the hand and her friend held on tightly.

"Everyone here will have heard of Mrs McIvett's comment by tomorrow," Lottie whispered in a shaky voice.

"And everyone will know the contempt with which we treated it. That woman is not worthy of another thought. You are worth a thousand of her."

"I do not think that is true." Lottie still looked on the brink of tears.

"Then you must take my word for it." She paused to allow Benjamin and Mr Nathaniel Fenbridge to catch up with them.

"Miss Harrington," Mr Nathaniel Fenbridge said with a smile. "This reel is one of my favourites. Would you be so kind as to dance with me?"

Amelia saw Lottie hesitate and squeezed her hand, giving a slight nod when Lottie glanced at her. The very best way to halt any more gossip was for Lottie to seen to be having a pleasant evening and not paying Mrs McIvett's words any mind.

Lottie fixed a smile on her face, where it sat over her distress like a mask, and allowed herself to be led once more onto the dance floor.

"Do you wish to dance?" Benjamin asked Amelia with his usual reluctance.

She laughed. "No. I will spare you that just now."

"Excellent."

"Thank you for not challenging Mrs McIvett to a duel."

He grinned and indicated his sling. "Well, I am not quite recovered from the last one but give me a day or two and who knows who I might challenge next."

*   *   *

Wrackley got into the carriage with a dreamy expression and Mr Brightford suppressed the urge to sigh with annoyance. His cousins had left in their own carriage so it was just the two of them. He had seen Wrackley running round after Miss Daventry tonight and guessed that he was another who had fallen prey to her charms.

He had seen her turn cool with a couple of her young admirers, casting them off without a backwards glance, but clearly Wrackley had enough wealth to be taken seriously.

He could not understand why a kind-hearted girl like Miss Harrington should suffer the miseries of a broken engagement and such cruel comments as the one she had endured earlier tonight, when a heartless creature like Miss Daventry had her pick of the best of the gentlemen.

Miss Daventry might be lovely - she was in fact the most beautiful woman he had ever seen - but last year he had overheard her intention to wed the wealthiest man she could find. He had been appalled to realise her so ruthless.

He liked Wrackley and, should it come to that, would pity him if he ended up married to someone so cold-hearted.

As if this thought had been his prompt, Wrackley looked up from his reverie with a smile and said in an awed tone, "Do you not think that Miss Daventry is the most beautiful and charming lady in existence?"

Brightford unhappily delivered the blow: "I regret to have to say that I have found that lady to be the most heartless, fortune-hunting schemer I have ever encountered."

The smile dropped from Wrackley's face.

The rest of the carriage journey went by in silence.

CHAPTER NINE

AMELIA WONDERED, as she lay in bed the morning after the ball, when Mr Wrackley would ask her to marry him.

Would he kneel down to propose? How ever he did it she was certain it would be the most romantic moment of her life.

They would be so happy together. It would be strange living in England instead of Scotland - she would greatly miss Lottie and her parents but they would all visit her often and she, them. She and Mr Wrackley would be able to visit London whenever they pleased, which would be bliss. She would visit the best modiste in London and would look so beautiful in her new clothes that, when he saw her, Mr Wrackley would exclaim in amazement…

Of course, he might not be wealthy enough for her to buy all the things she had spent years imagining or to visit all the places she had heard of. She had no idea whether he was rich or no better off than her own parents. Unbelievably, she did not care.

She understood now why Lottie had spoken of falling in love as if nothing else mattered. Amelia just wanted a lifetime with Mr Wrackley. She giggled as she realised she did not even know his first name.

How strange life was, and how perfect.

* * *

"Have you heard the news about Mr Saverney?"

They were strolling in the garden behind Benjamin's home. His heart - which had bloomed at the arrival of Mr Nathaniel Fenbridge - sunk down towards his stomach. The words had been spoken hesitantly and he feared the worst. "What has the skunk done now?"

"He and his family have left Edinburgh. Brightford heard from friends of his mother that they will be spending time at their country estate and will likely not return this year."

Benjamin took in this news with pleasure. "My sister will be relieved not to have to worry about seeing him and perhaps the gossip about the broken engagement will finally fade away. Thank you for informing me of this."

"Brightford was going to tell you himself but, when I said I wished to drop by, he allowed me to share the news." He took a step closer and Benjamin's heart once more became erratic. "I hope this will be the start of happier times for your family."

"I have nothing to complain of for myself. I am pleased to have had the opportunity to make your acquaintance." The words were inadequate – conveying but a fraction of his feelings on the matter – but brought a sunny smile to Mr Fenbridge's face.

"As am I."

"Has Brightford showed you around Edinburgh to your satisfaction? I would be happy to escort you in any further sight-seeing you wish to do."

"I appreciate that. It is more the countryside outside the city I am curious to see."

"We could go riding?" Benjamin suggested, keen for as

much of Mr Fenbridge's company as could be achieved. "Perhaps take a picnic. There are some excellent views from some of the nearby hills."

"That sounds perfect. It is a lovely dry day today..."

Benjamin nodded in agreement. "I will have our cook prepare some food to take and, while that is being done, perhaps you will tell me more of your brother's estate."

"Gladly."

* * *

Amelia heard footsteps on the stairs and remembered with pleasure that Lottie was due to call. Suddenly she could not wait to tell her friend all about Mr Wrackley. She had waited because she wanted to be certain of her feelings but now it seemed incomprehensible that she had ever had any doubts.

There was a knock on her door and the maid announced Lottie, who then entered.

Amelia - who had been sitting on a chair in the library reading a romance aloud to her cat - got to her feet. She smiled at Lottie then looked closely at her, concerned. "You are pale - are you ill?"

"No, I am well." They both sat down. "It was foolish of me but I lay awake after the ball thinking of Mrs McIvett's insult."

With a pang of guilt, Amelia realised she had entirely forgotten about this. "She is just a silly, spiteful woman and does not deserve a second thought."

"Others might have been too polite to speak as she did but how many were thinking something similar?"

"You must not think like that. You must forget the past and think that likely the happiest years of your life are all ahead of you."

Lottie bit her lip. "Apparently Mr Saverney and his family have left to stay at their country estate, probably for the rest of the year."

"That is excellent news." Amelia said, happy that he had finally had the good sense to know where he was not wanted. "All the more reason for you to make a resolution to start anew."

Lottie nodded. "Now that Benjy is recovering I will try to do so."

"You are long overdue for happiness and you will find it soon, I am certain."

Lottie gave a smile, at once looking more like her old self.

"I have some good news I hope you will be pleased about," Amelia said. "I am in love."

"With whom?" Lottie asked, eyes lighting up, then guessed, "Mr Wrackley?"

"Yes. Every time I have seen him he has been attentive and admiring, last night most of all. We talked all evening and he never took his eyes off me. It was perfect. I am sure he will propose soon."

"That is wonderful. I am so happy for you."

Amelia saw that Lottie really meant this and suddenly felt sick as she recalled her own reaction to Lottie's engagement. She had always known that Lottie was a better person than her but she had never wanted to correct her own shortcomings before. It did not seem fair that Amelia should be on the verge such joy when Lottie had endured such misery.

"Tell me more," Lottie begged, animated.

"It makes me so happy just to be near him. I have never felt such things," Amelia confessed. "It scares me at times."

"I could not be more glad for you. Do your parents know how you feel?"

"I believe my mother knows I have a preference for him but I doubt she has guessed that I love him. Do you think I should say something to them?"

"I am sure you know best, but it might be awkward if

Mr Wrackley called to ask your father for his permission to marry you and your father did not know that you would welcome it."

"Indeed you are right. I will speak to them today."

"I am sure they will be delighted."

"I hope so. I have no idea of the size of Mr Wrackley's estate or of his wealth or otherwise and, Lottie, I do not care."

Lottie was, of course, well acquainted with her feelings on the matter of money, and looked suitably astonished. "How extraordinary."

"I know. I always used to think I was so sensible but such considerations seem unimportant next to my love for him."

Lottie seemed in a far more cheerful mood when she left and Amelia wished with all her heart that Lottie might soon meet a good man who would make up for all this year's disappointments.

Amelia hoped she would see Mr Wrackley the next day - she could not bear the thought of any time apart from him.

* * *

The weather was ideal for the excursion. Benjamin and Mr Nathaniel Fenbridge had ridden at a good pace for several hours and now stopped, in a spot Benjamin recommended, to look down over the city and surrounding countryside while they ate the excellent picnic Mrs McInty had put together for them.

The day was a hot one, the sunshine brightening the green of the long wild grass and the yellows and pinks of the gorse and wild flowers amongst it. They sat in the shade of an oak tree and Benjamin could not think that he had ever been more content.

Mr Fenbridge sat on the grass on the far side of the

picnic cloth with a glass of ale in his hand. "Was your sister glad to know that Mr Saverney is gone from the city?"

"She was relieved and, once she has been able to talk it all over with Amelia - Miss Daventry, I mean - I believe she will be more like her old cheerful self."

"If I may ask an impertinent question, do you believe she still loves him?"

"I should hope not," he exclaimed then considered the question more seriously. "My sister does not easily talk of her feelings but I believe that Mr Saverney's character has been revealed to such a disadvantage that she cannot still love him. Indeed I think she only ever loved the man he pretended to be."

"Then in time perhaps she will think she was lucky not to have married him?"

"I am sure of it. It is more other people's comments that are difficult for her at present. She is a gentle sensitive girl and nothing could be more painful to her than being at the centre of such unpleasant gossip, even though she is blameless in the matter. I can only be grateful she has Miss Daventry to help her through it - Amelia is better for her than any of her family."

"I am sure you underestimate yourself," Fenbridge said quietly, eyes fixed on Benjamin's face.

"She knows I love her but I think I caused her more anguish than relief fighting that stupid duel. Amelia is like a sister to her - to both of us really - and she treats the gossip with the contempt it deserves."

"I saw the put-down she gave the lady who made a cruel comment to your sister at the last ball. She seemed a most loyal friend."

"The best."

"And what of you? Do you have many close friends?"

Benjamin kept his gaze fixed on the view ahead of him. His heart told him to explain why he had lost his friends but his head said that all would be ruined if he did so. "I have many acquaintances but the men I used to think I could tell anything to… It turned out not to be the case. They found me… more complicated than they had thought and did not like the discovery."

"I believe we are all of us complicated. Perhaps younger men worry too much about being the same as their fellows.

"I am the person I am. It is difficult to hide it."

Fenbridge gave a frown. "You should not have to hide anything, not at least from those close to you."

Benjamin turned to look at Fenbridge, the words of who he was on the tip of his tongue, but his courage failed him. "Shall we ride further out or head back?"

* * *

It was rare to see Mr Daventry at the private club as he was not a betting man. Although they were perfectly amiable acquaintances, it was even more rare for him to seek out Brightford himself.

The two men greeted each other and ordered drinks as they exchanged pleasantries about mutual friends and the unusually long dry spell in the weather recently. Mr Daventry, never one for prevarication, then said, "I wonder if you could tell me about the character of Mr Wrackley. He has been showing an interest in my daughter, Amelia, and, since he is not a local man, I know nothing of him."

Brightford wondered, with a touch of guilt, if Wrackley's interest would be as strong after his own warning about Miss Daventry. He told himself he would have been a poor friend if he had not spoken. If Wrackley was actually in love with her then he would likely still pursue her, regardless of what anyone else said. If not then it was better all round for him to back away. At least, that was what he told himself. "Mr Wrackley is an excellent man, sensible and good-natured. He is not a great gambler and his behaviour with women of every class is gentlemanly."

"I am delighted to hear that, sir," Huntly said with a nod. "Thank you for speaking to me so frankly on the matter."

Brightford did not feel he was owed any gratitude from Huntly; quite the contrary. He abruptly wished he had never spoken to Wrackley about Miss Daventry but surely Wrackley would not take his words too much to heart?

CHAPTER TEN

IT WAS BENJAMIN and Mr Nathaniel Fenbridge who suggested the idea, then Lottie mentioned it to Amelia who at once began making arrangements. Two days later the party of six set out in two carriages to visit the formal gardens of Edinburgh Castle, taking a large picnic with them. It was another balmy day - indeed she could remember few such fine summers - but Amelia's happiness turned to acute disappointment at the realisation that Mr Wrackley was not taking part in the expedition. She had been so certain of seeing him again and had accordingly taken two hours trying on different outfits to ensure she was looking her best, so the news, conveyed by Mr Alexander Fenbridge, that Mr Wrackley had business in the city was a great blow. He was a stranger to Edinburgh - how could he have such pressing business that would keep him from her side?

She was sharing a carriage with just Lottie - the four men in the other conveyance - so she could express her feelings aloud.

"I am sure he would not have stayed in Edinburgh had it not been absolutely necessary," Lottie said to her. "He is an important man with his own estate to run. He likely received a letter about his estate that he had to attend to immediately, or something else of that nature."

Amelia nodded at the sense in this. "But I had so wanted to see him and for you to see how perfectly matched we are."

"I am certain there will be countless occasions in the future for that."

Lottie was in a cheerful mood and that was pleasant to see but Amelia wished that they might both be in good humour at the same time just once. It seemed that in the last few months there had always been something occurring to vex or upset one of them, usually Lottie. Still, Lottie was right that this was just a brief disappointment, nothing more sinister, so she would not ruin the expedition for her friend by being downcast.

They arrived at the destination, made polite comments about the stunning gardens then enjoyed the sunshine while a footman laid out the picnic. Amelia waved to Lottie who was standing at the river and had gestured to her to look at the family of swans gliding by.

"I saw a pheasant stalking about near the trees if you are interested in birdlife," Mr Nathaniel Fenbridge said, appearing at her side, his eyes also upon the river.

"I do like to see various birds and mammals living their lives. They seem more restful than people somehow."

"That sounds like something Jolly would say, only with more of a scathing tone towards humanity."

"Who?" An absurd thought struck her. "You cannot mean Mr Brightford?"

"It is an old nickname," Mr Nathaniel Fenbridge said, eyes twinkling with amusement.

"And an ironic one unless he is much changed."

His mouth twitched. "I should not reveal this..."

She stepped closer to him, leaning forward to listen.

"... But he was in fact worse as a child."

She gasped. "I would not have thought it possible."

"He was the kind of child who disapproved of pranks

and who told tales on any trouble Alex or myself got into."

"I can picture it clearly." A miniature Brightford, smaller but with just the same condescending frown. "Did your relations force you to spend a lot of time with him?"

"Not too much but we certainly did not look forward to the visits." He gave a contagious laugh.

"Worse than he is now." It hardly bore thinking about. She had certainly never met a man more critical and prone to disapproval. It was unfair of him too because, with his wealth and good family name, he would otherwise be a good catch for some young lady.

"Do not misunderstand me," he said, interrupting her thoughts. "I am fond of him now and he has acknowledged that he was unbearable. He might still have that disapproving look about him…"

"Certainly whenever he observes me!"

"… But he is a good, kind man underneath it."

"Indeed?" She could not help injecting a note of doubt over this assessment.

"I can assure you of it."

They headed to where the picnic was set up in the shade of a beech tree and Amelia could not help glancing at Mr Brightford and considering what Mr Nathaniel Fenbridge had said. He was an attractive man, she observed, trying to be fair in her assessment, tall and slender but with a definite strength to him. He did not dress as handsomely as Mr Wrackley, of course, nor have such charm and really the way he frowned all the time was highly irritating…

She gave up trying to make in impartial assessment of him and went to find Lottie who was strolling towards them with Mr Alexander Fenbridge, laughing at something he had said. The sight was such a rare one in recent times that Amelia paused, smiling, to see her friend so happy. The two of them caught up with her and she could not help saying to Lottie, "Has Mr Fenbridge told you of the nickname he and Mr Nathaniel Fenbridge have for their cousin?"

* * *

"Mr Wrackley!"

Amelia had not thought to see him when she had rode to the shops, just her maid, Walker, with her, to have the heel from one of a pair of dance slippers repaired. It was the day after the expedition, which had been a lovely day and, Amelia thought, it had done Lottie good to get away from the opinions and censure of Edinburgh society.

As always the sight of Mr Wrackley left her nearly breathless and agitated. He was impeccably dressed as always and she could not imagine any other man being so handsome. She curtsied as she sought something to say.

"Miss Daventry." He bowed to her but his tone was lifeless and his expression serious.

"Is everything well? Mr Alexander Fenbridge said that you had business in the city. I hope it was not unsuccessful?"

"No." He glanced away. "The, er, matter is settled perfectly well. Was your outing pleasant?"

"Very much so, but we were all sorry that you missed it."

"As was I." He touched his watch fob then let his hand fall away in a restless manner. "Forgive me, but I must return to Brightford's house or I will be late."

He was gone almost before she could curtsy, striding away without a backwards glance and she stared after him in dismay. What could have prompted him to behave so coldly towards her? Perhaps her behaviour at the ball had been too forward or he had met someone he liked better. She felt ill at such thoughts, her hopes for a future with him falling apart.

She could not get the hard expression on his face out of her head. He had not smiled at her once.

* * *

Lottie sighed and wished her life could somehow magically change.

Yesterday had been a beautiful day - she could not have asked for anything better. The weather had been sunny, the countryside beautiful and the gentlemen had been polite and friendly but not over-solicitous in the way that always made her uncomfortable.

She had returned home feeling that perhaps she could finally put Mr Saverney behind her, but at the shops with her mother there had yet again been whispers in her direction and amused looks. Was she really the most interesting source of gossip for the whole of Edinburgh society? She kept thinking with longing of returning to the countryside where no one knew what had happened to her but her family would not do this for several months. She felt she had been thrown into a sophisticated world this year that she did not know how to handle: she enjoyed dancing at balls but flirtatious compliments embarrassed her and she spent half her time acutely aware of how awkward she was in comparison with Amelia.

However, when Mr Wrackley proposed to Amelia that would take Lottie's mind off it all and give her something good to focus on. She wondered how soon he would do so. She had never doubted that Amelia would get engaged this season, her friend's beauty and confidence always winning admirers and she was delighted that Amelia had found a man she could love, not merely respect. Amelia would be so happy...

* * *

Amelia arrived at Lottie's house to visit her just as Mr Nathaniel Fenbridge was leaving, presumably after seeing Benjamin. They paused to briefly greet each other on the steps outside. Having done so he began to walk away and, on impulse, she said his name, stopping him. When he turned back she swallowed nervously.

"Mr Fenbridge, do you know if I have perhaps done something to offend Mr Wrackley?" She felt embarrassed mentioning it, knowing it was improper to do so, but might never get another chance to speak to him alone and she had to find out what had gone wrong between herself and Mr Wrackley. If she knew what was wrong she might be able to mend it.

His brow furrowed in concern and he said gently, "I fear that he has not taken me into his confidence on the subject."

"You do not think…" She hesitated then said quickly, blushing, "You do not think he could have misunderstood my friendship with you?"

He smiled as if she had made a joke. "He would never think that. Wrackley knows that I, er, am not the marrying kind."

"Oh!" she exclaimed, delighted. "Then you and Mr Harrington …" She covered her mouth with her hand as she realised the extent of her indiscretion.

However, Mr Fenbridge did not look in the least offended, simply remarking, "I did not realise that young ladies, as a rule, knew of such things."

"We do not," she said contritely, "and we certainly never speak of them."

He laughed. "Well, then let us simply say that I have hopes that Mr Harrington and myself will be able to remain close friends for the rest of our lives."

"I am so glad."

He paused then said, "Would you like me to try to ascertain why Mr Wrackley's behaviour towards you has changed?" When she bit her lip he added, "I will be discreet."

She smiled, liking him more than ever and glad that she had taken him into her confidence. "Thank you."

She then sought Lottie out upstairs and was instantly asked whether she had received a proposal from Mr Wrackley. She forced a smile onto her face as she demurred.

* * *

Nathan dealt out the cards to Brightford and Alex then, just because Brightford finally had a decent hand, got up and crossed the room to where Wrackley was sitting with a book in his hands. Wrackley was never much of a reader and, as far as Brightford had noticed, had not turned a page in the last hour.

"I could not help observing that you treated Miss Daventry in a somewhat cool manner yesterday." Fenbridge said quietly.

Brightford looked at the cards in his hand but they faded from his vision as he listened to the conversation on the other side of the drawing room.

Wrackley said shortly, "Without meaning any offence, Nathan, how is that your concern?"

"I like the young lady and would not wish to see her distressed."

Alex prompted Brightford to call and he did so automatically, no longer caring whether he won or lost the game.

"You know her as little as I do. I behaved as I did yesterday as I did not wish Miss Daventry to misunderstand my intentions. I think her lovely but not someone my family would approve of my marrying." After this speech Wrackley strode from the room and Nathan joined them to finally play the already dealt game of cards, although his expression remained troubled.

"I was not aware that you were more than slightly acquainted with Miss Daventry," Brightford commented, moving suits around in his hand.

"I have run into her a couple of times at Harrington's household. We have conversed and I think highly of her."

"Then I believe you have been deceived," Brightford felt encumbered to point out. "As far as I can see, the chit is utterly mercenary in her pursuit of a wealthy husband."

"You cannot fault her for that," Alex said, weighing into the conversation on his brother's side. He threw away a card and Nathan picked one up from the pack. "Her family is relatively poor so it is her duty to marry well. You would not fault a man for pursuing a wealthy woman to help his family and his inheritance, would you?"

"That is different. One expects a delicately reared young lady to behave with more innocence, to behave more like Miss Harrington, for example."

"You criticize her for being intelligent then?" Nathan teased, adding, "She is the heiress to the estate whereas Miss Harrington has a brother to take care of her. Miss Daventry has more responsibility."

Brightford snorted, amazed that Nathan of all people could have been taken in by a pretty face. A pretty female face. "If that young woman has ever thought of anything beyond her own pleasure I will eat my hat."

"Then you should do so," Nathan said. "I know for a fact straight from Benj - from Harrington that she has constantly supported Miss Harrington through the unpleasant business with Mr Saverney. Harrington says Miss Daventry has done all she can to lift Miss Harrington's spirits and, indeed, he clearly thinks of her fondly, almost like another sister, himself."

Brightford stared at Nathan in shock.

"It is your turn," Alex reminded him and Brightford picked up and card and threw it down again without so much as looking at it.

This was a side to Miss Daventry he had never

imagined and, now that he thought about it, he could recall instances of her defending or being protective of Miss Harrington. Could he have misjudged Miss Daventry?

* * *

"How is Charlotte lately?" Mrs Daventry asked over a quiet family dinner served by their footman, the occasion an informal one compared to the grand dinner parties they had been attending over the last few months.

"She is well enough," Amelia said, frowning as she thought of how weary Lottie had looked today, "but after every unhappiness she has endured this year it is as if a light inside her has been extinguished."

"She needs a husband," Mrs Daventry said. "You both do."

Amelia thought of Mr Wrackley with a pang of sadness then with a determination to speak to him and resolve whatever was wrong between them.

"I will speak to Mr Brightford," Mr Daventry said.

Amelia dropped her spoon into her soup and stared at her father. He thought Mr Brightford wished to marry her? The idea gave her a peculiar surge of pleasure but it made little sense. She checked: "You want me to marry Mr Brightford?"

"No, no. I meant Miss Harrington."

Amelia recalled Mr Brightford's attentiveness towards Lottie at the recent balls and her stomach lurched. He was not right for Lottie; not in the least. They would both be miserable. "What makes you think he has a particular liking for Lottie?"

"He is a sensible man and she is a sensible girl. It would be an excellent match and he is the right age to settle down. I will suggest it to him."

Relief flooded Amelia. As if suggesting such a reason as that would possibly work. She recalled her own reaction to the idea of marrying Mr Brightford with puzzlement and some consternation. No, that had been her ego: of course it would be a great honour to be courted by so powerful and wealthy a man as Mr Brightford but that was all. She did not even like him and, of course, she was in love with Mr Wrackley.

Mr Brightford and she – what a ridiculous idea!

CHAPTER ELEVEN

"YOU WILL NEVER believe my news."

Lottie's expression held a nervous excitement that was quite unlike her and, after a moment's confusion, Amelia recalled her father's words about arranging a marriage between Lottie and Mr Brightford. Her heart fell. It was impossible. This must be something else.

Amelia gestured for Lottie to take the seat opposite her in the small sewing room, as she asked with trepidation, "What has happened?"

"I am engaged once more."

Amelia could not speak. She had never fainted in her life but thought she might be about to do so. That would explain her peculiar feeling of misery and the sudden chill in the room on a warm summer's day.

"I can understand your shock," Lottie went on, misunderstanding Amelia's silence. She spoke nervously as if anticipating an objection. "I never expected it and, of course, I have only known Mr Alexander Fenbridge for a matter of weeks…"

"Mr Fenbridge has proposed to you?" Suddenly Amelia found she could breathe again and she had to blink back tears of relief.

"Yes," Lottie confirmed, clearly concerned about Amelia's reaction. "I cannot even say I have fallen in love, so I know it must make no sense at all to you, but I like him a great deal and this seems to me the best way to recover from the damage to my reputation. You do like Mr Fenbridge, do you not?"

"Oh, yes," Amelia reassured her. "Very much. He has always been kind and thoughtful. I think it a highly sensible match." The sort of match she herself would have wanted before meeting Mr Wrackley. "However, Lottie, you have always believed so strongly in marrying for love."

"I know. Yet, having accepted him, I feel such relief and gratitude. I am certain it is the right decision."

Amelia did not want to take away Lottie's unexpected happiness but felt she must ask, "What if you married him then fell in love with someone else?"

"What if I did not marry him and ended up an old maid? My parents could not bear that and nor could I. I have seen couples who married for love but were still not happy and others who married for practical reasons but developed a strong affection for each other. I cannot predict the future but I believe I will have a husband I can respect and care about and that is all I ask."

She seemed genuinely happy about the decision and, as she had said, marriage to a good man who cared about her was better than no marriage. "As long as you are certain this is what you want to do then I am happy for you."

Lottie's face lit up in a warm smile. "Thank you. I am so glad you are not opposed to it. Now when Mr Wrackley proposes to you we can be married at almost the same time. Our husbands will even be friends so we will be able to visit each other very frequently."

Amelia forced a smile, wishing she had not expressed such certainty that Mr Wrackley would propose. Everything that had seemed simple suddenly seemed so confusing. She had always been the practical one but faced with Lottie making a sensible marriage and having to live with the consequences of the decision for the rest of her life, Amelia was afraid for her friend. She herself loved Mr Wrackley so why then had she reacted in such an emotional manner to the prospect of Lottie marrying Mr Brightford?

* * *

"What a pleasant surprise," Mr Nathaniel Fenbridge said when the butler led Benjamin into the library to see him at Mr Brightford's house. He put down his book and smiled with a warmth that made Benjamin automatically return it, his mood lifted just by seeing the other man. "What brings you here?"

"My sister has informed me that she has accepted your brother's offer of marriage."

Mr Fenbridge gestured for him to take a seat in one of the chairs that had been upholstered in the same vibrant green patterned cloth as the curtains. "You are not unhappy about the announcement?"

"No, not at all. Your brother has always seemed likeable and a good man to me, but he is not local and my sister has been through a lot this year. I just… I wanted to be certain that he will try to make her happy. Forgive me the impertinence of the question…"

"There is nothing to forgive." Mr Fenbridge's blue eyes were warm. "I can completely understand your concerns and I hope I can remove them. My brother is a kind man, a little reserved but I can promise that he has the very greatest affection for Miss Harrington and will do all he can to give her a good life."

"Thank you. You have indeed reassured me." He felt the need to apologise again, afraid that he might have damaged their friendship and unable to bear the idea. "Lottie is my only sister…"

"I promise I am not offended."

Benjamin gave a relieved nod. "Good. I would never want that."

"Nor I. Indeed, I am hoping that since I live on my brother's estate this change of circumstances will mean we will see each other frequently in the future."

Benjamin felt his face grow warm, pleased by the affection in the words and embarrassed at just how much they meant to him. "I would like that very much."

When he left Mr Brightford's home a little while later Benjamin wondered if Mr Fenbridge could possibly return his romantic feelings. The man's words had certainly indicated a strong regard for his company but perhaps Benjamin was just reading into them what he most wished for. He had had infatuations before but nothing like the depth of feeling he felt for Fenbridge.

Recalling the result of speaking of the subject before, he could not risk saying something and being wrong. The thought of Fenbridge looking at him with disgust and dislike made him feel ill. On the other hand, the idea that Fenbridge might indeed feel the same way…

This uncertainty could drive a man mad. He nudged his horse into a trot, leading the animal towards an area of countryside where he could gallop freely and work off some of his agitation.

* * *

Amelia stared out of the sewing room window, the view of the garden outside a lovely one, but her mind on a view of the future that was not lovely at all.

It was only after Lottie left that Amelia remembered that Mr Alexander Fenbridge's estate was in some part of England countless miles away. Lottie would always have family in Edinburgh so Amelia had told herself Lottie would often visit them so Amelia would see her then.

However, aside from a visit of perhaps a month per year Amelia would not see her; she would lose her best friend. Amelia might be able to visit Lottie's new home at first but would it be possible to continue doing so after she herself married, assuming that that ever happened?

Amelia used to fantasise about travelling with her husband to exotic places such as London and Paris and all the fashionable luxuries she would be able to buy, but she had never once considered what she might have to give up as an adult. She had known Lottie for virtually her whole life and the thought of suddenly losing her was horrible. Of course, she thought with a heavy sigh, she herself might never marry then she could visit Lottie as often as possible until Lottie and Mr Fenbridge were sick of her.

Amelia made a groan of frustration at her thoughts and threw down her embroidery. She would take Walker to the shops and spend more money than was prudent and then she would feel better.

Satisfied with this decision, she put it into effect, although by the time she got to the shops they had lost much of their appeal. Still, she found some French lace which she bought as an engagement gift for Lottie and called at Mr Harrington's house to give it to her.

She walked into Lottie's room and, before she could say so much as a greeting, Lottie burst out, "What if Mr Fenbridge jilts me?"

Amelia stared at her in surprise that changed to dismay at how badly Lottie was still affected by Mr Saverney's treatment of her. "That is impossible."

"Is it?" Lottie paced up and down the small space between her four-poster bed and large oak wardrobe. "What if the fault was not with Mr Saverney but with me? Perhaps I am just not loveable."

"Nonsense! Mr Saverney was a weak man who behaved abominably to you, but it could never happen again…"

"…I am not so certain…"

"… Well, I am. How did Mr Fenbridge seem when you

accepted his proposal? Happy?"

"Yes." Lottie paused and her expression became calmer. "He was pleased and happy."

"There, then. Your fear was understandable but it was also wrong, I promise you."

Lottie smiled. "What would I do without your friendship?"

"We will both find out when you are living all the way down in some distant part of England," Amelia blurted out in what she was sure was a self-pitying tone.

"Now who is talking nonsense," Lottie said calmly. "I will spend half my time here visiting my family and you will spend half your time staying with me and we will see each other just as often as we do now."

Amelia nodded, allowing herself to be comforted by the idea and denying the doubts at the back of her mind.

CHAPTER TWELVE

IT WAS EARLY morning and Mr Brightford viewed the chests being loaded onto Mr Wrackley's coach with concern then walked back inside to find him. Wrackley was in the dining room taking his leave of Nathan and Alex.

"I thought you had intended to stay here until the end of the season," Brightford said, with an unpleasant idea of where this change of plans had come from.

"We have already made the same comment," Nathan told him, long legs folding at the ankles as he looked up from a dining chair at the two men.

"I simply feel I should not leave my estate for any longer. My sisters will also be glad to have me home." Wrackley fidgeted with his gloves as he spoke and the look Nathan threw Brightford said he did not believe a word of this.

"Has someone offended you in some way?" he queried.

Wrackley smiled. "Of course not, old friend. I could not have been made more at home here."

"Does this have anything to do with Miss Daventry?" Nathan ventured.

When Wrackley looked away and failed to answer this,

Brightford said, "Perhaps I should never have spoken to you of her. I thought you deserved a warning but maybe it was an unwanted intrusion into a private matter that did not concern me."

"Not at all. I will admit that I admired Miss Daventry when I first met her but, for my family's sake, it is necessary for my future wife to be of superior character and morality and it is clear Miss Daventry is not suitable after all. I am grateful to you for not allowing me to make a mistake I would have regretted."

"What exactly did Jolly say?" Nathan asked, frowning.

Brightford recalled his words with a twinge of conscience as Wrackley said, "It is not important. Being a stranger to Edinburgh, I allowed myself to be deceived by a lovely face."

"I like Miss Daventry and have found nothing in her character to dislike," Nathan said.

"I, too, have found her most amiable," Alex agreed from the other side of the dining table.

"But neither of you know anything of Miss Daventry and her family beyond a handful of brief encounters," Wrackley said. "Brightford knows her character far better so I must accept his greater knowledge."

"Perhaps if we sat down and discussed this in a sensible manner…" Nathan began but Wrackley shook his head and cut across his words.

"… I fear I have made a fool of myself and also given Miss Daventry false hopes of my intentions. It is best for everyone if I leave. She will doubtless find a wealthy man to marry without me here and…" He grimaced. "Honestly, that is not something I could bear to watch." He patted Nathan's arm. "I will see you and Alex when you return home and, Jolly, I hope you will come and stay with me in the near future and allow me to return your excellent hospitality."

With a final tense smile to them all he turned and strode out of the house. They followed more slowly and waved goodbye as his carriage pulled away.

When it was out of sight Nathan turned to Brightford and said in an unusually cool tone, "Perhaps you had better explain exactly what you said to Wrackley and how you justified your interference…"

* * *

"You are leaving now?" Amelia said, horrified. She had resigned herself to Lottie going but had thought it would not be for months. They had only been engaged a matter of days. How was this even possible?

"Not for a week." Lottie looked excited at the prospect, which made Amelia feel even more abandoned. "My parents and I will travel with Mr Alexander Fenbridge to his estate so he can introduce me to his married sisters. We will remain there and be married in about two months."

"Why must it be so soon?" Amelia complained. "Why can you not remain for the rest of the Edinburgh season?"

"It was actually me who asked for the wedding to take place as soon as possible. I want to meet Mr Fenbridge's other siblings and see his home and begin my married life."

"And marry before he can change his mind?"

"No." Lottie smiled. "That was a moment of foolishness and you helped put such fears from my mind. Edinburgh society has just lost its appeal to me. All I care about here are my family and you. My parents will be with me for the next few months and Benjamin will escort you and your parents in a month's time. Mr Fenbridge and I will marry, go for our honeymoon and then return to Edinburgh to bring you back to stay with us again, if you are willing, and if are not married yourself by then."

"I will gladly stay with you on both occasions," Amelia said, cheered by this demonstration that she was still an important part of Lottie's life. "And it certainly does not seem as if I shall be married for the foreseeable future."

"You have not seen Mr Wrackley lately?"

"Not for two weeks. Perhaps he has met someone else."

"Then he is a feckless fool," Lottie declared, "and you are well rid of him."

Amelia was just leaving when she once again ran into Mr Nathaniel Fenbridge, who seemed to spend as much time here as she did. They paused in the hall to greet each other and she offered her congratulations on his brother's marriage.

"I am delighted for him," he responded cheerfully. "Miss Harrington is admirable in every way and I am sure the pair are well suited."

She nodded, hoping his assessment would prove correct. Striving for a tone of casual enquiry, she said, "Will Mr Wrackley be returning home when Mr Alexander Fenbridge leaves or will he remain in Edinburgh for a while?"

"You have not heard?" Mr Fenbridge frowned. "Wrackley left two days ago."

"Oh." It should not make a difference: he had clearly changed his mind about her. The blow should not have struck so hard but, without even knowing it, she had still had hope that all could be resolved between them.

"Perhaps it is unfair of me to reveal this but I know he admired you greatly but was persuaded that your interest in him was entirely mercenary."

"He believed the gossip of some stranger…"

"It was not a stranger."

Mr Fenbridge looked uncomfortable and Amelia returned his gaze blankly. Who would Mr Wrackley trust who knew her at all? The second blow was just as painful as the first: "Mr Brightford."

CHAPTER THIRTEEN

LOTTIE CAME TO see Amelia on the morning she was due to leave, dressed in a new grey and blue travelling outfit that made her look like an elegant stranger.

"I was going to visit you to wave you goodbye," Amelia protested as they sat down either side of her bedroom window. She was only just dressed and her black curls were still around her shoulders.

"I knew if you did that I would burst into tears and I do not want Mr Fenbridge to see me in such a state, although there is probably no getting around it as I will still have to say goodbye to Benjy which will doubtless have the same effect. At least Mr Nathaniel Fenbridge is staying to keep him company until you all join us at Mr Fenbridge's estate."

"It will be your estate as well soon."

"Yes." Lottie smiled, bright-eyed in anticipation of the adventures ahead. "I am so excited to see it. You know how much I like the countryside - I know I will be happy there."

"Well, you will be sorely missed here. The last events of the season will be very dull without your presence."

"I am sure you will have countless handsome men to

dance with and will enjoy them very well."

Amelia tried to smile and failed. "I doubt it."

"Mr Wrackley is a fool for losing his chance with you. Perhaps you will meet someone when you come to see us and we will live close by again."

"What an excellent notion." The idea had appeal even if only for that reason but she no longer had the heart for finding a husband. Amelia had not told Lottie that it was Mr Brightford who had sabotaged her relationship with Mr Wrackley. It had not seemed fair since Mr Brightford and Mr Alexander Fenbridge were related and she did not want a rift in the family; besides that, it was too painful to talk about.

Lottie took Amelia's hand in her own gloved one. "It will all resolve itself for the best. Remember how unhappy I was just a short time ago and now I could not be in better spirits. When we see each other again, things will likely already have come right for you and you will have the country at your feet."

Amelia could not help but laugh. "Another pleasant notion."

Once Lottie was gone, though, her good humour at once left her. Losing her best friend made everything else twice as hard to bear. Mr Wrackley was gone. Mr Brightford had the very lowest opinion of her and it had caused him to take away her best chance at future happiness. No, she would not think of it; any of it. She called for Walker to come and dress her hair so she could go out and distract herself.

* * *

It was mid-morning when she decided to call at Mr Harrington's depleted household to see how Benjamin was. She had spent the morning admiring cloth and trying on hats she could not afford to buy and her mood was lower than ever. The prospect of a dinner party that evening did nothing to cheer her, not when her best friend would never again attend such events with her. She could barely recall a time before she and Lottie had been friends and it seemed almost impossible that Lottie should suddenly be absent from her life.

Benjamin looked equally depressed when she was admitted to the library, prompting her to ask, "Are you missing your family already?"

His mouth twisted into something that was not a smile. "My father's parting words to me were that he expected me to be engaged to be married the next time he saw me and I was welcome to bring my future bride and her family with me to Lottie's wedding."

She felt a wave of sympathy, realising her own life was not the only one in chaos and at least she had her parents' support. "Will you do it? Propose to someone?"

He paced over to the window then back again. "I do not know. I am not sure I can live such a fake life, but if I do not do as he says…"

"You think he would disinherit you?"

"Yes."

She had always thought Mr Harrington a cold, stern man but this was heartless beyond belief. Why should he be so determined to deny his own son happiness? "Have you had a chance to tell Mr Nathaniel Fenbridge about this yet?"

"No. It is not his problem."

"He cares about you, perhaps in the same way that you care about him."

His eyes shot to her face, gaze searching. "Do you think so?"

"I do. Between the two of you I am sure you can think of a solution to this."

She returned home feeling that at least if her own life was not what she might wish then at least she had offered some excellent advice to a friend. From Mr Nathaniel

Fenbridge's words in the past she was positive he felt the same way as Benjamin and she was fond of them both so it would be good to see them happy.

* * *

Brightford stared out of the dining room window at the dappled sunshine that fell through the various trees in his garden creating areas of bright light and shadow, bright colours and dull ones. His house seemed empty after Alex's departure. Nathan was still around but he was out a lot and he was still angry with Brightford over Miss Daventry. The anger was rare in someone normally so good-natured and it once again caused Brightford to question whether his judgement of Miss Daventry had been right and whether he should have kept quiet to Wrackley.

But surely he knew Miss Daventry better than Nathan did? He had always found her outspoken opinions irritating but he recalled now that he had been quite taken by her beauty the first few times he had seen her. Overhearing her cool intention to find a wealthy man had shocked him and killed any attraction. However, the callousness he had attributed to her did not match the affectionate behaviour towards Miss Harrington that Fenbridge had described and he himself had seen her rise hotly to her friend's defence when Miss Harrington had been insulted at a ball.

Perhaps when he had overheard her a year ago she had been too young to know what she wanted and her views had changed. Perhaps she genuinely had cared about Wrackley.

Perhaps she had cared only for his wealth.

He shook his head in frustration at his circular thoughts and decided that he would get nowhere at the moment. As he left the house and headed for his stables he decided to observe Miss Daventry more carefully in future and if it turned out that he had been in the wrong then… well, he would think of some way to put things right.

* * *

Amelia's words had given Benjamin more hope than he had dared have before. Surely if she - someone who could see the situation impartially - thought Mr Nathaniel Fenbridge returned his feelings then it must be true?

The two men had taken one of their rides - a regular tradition between them now - into the countryside. They had now paused to eat a light lunch, their horses munching companionably on the grass beside them.

"The view here is lovely," Fenbridge said, sprawled on the soft grass beside him, close enough to kiss.

Benjamin stared sightlessly around him, pulse racing, thinking of what he wanted to say and trying to build up his confidence. "Yes. Most pleasant."

"You seem a little distracted."

"I have been forced to consider my future and in particular marriage." He paused, trying to find the right words to convey his hopes for their relationship.

"I nearly became engaged some years ago."

These quietly spoken words hit Benjamin like a blow and he stared at his companion in growing shock. He wished he could never have heard this and go back to his previous state of hope but it was too late. "What was her name?"

Fenbridge looked surprised at the question, as if his mind had been elsewhere. "Miss McLeod."

"I suppose she was attractive and accomplished?"

"Yes. Both."

Of course she was, Benjamin thought bitterly. What a spectacular fool he had been. Fenbridge was only a bachelor because this Miss McLeod had broken his heart. Benjamin's only consolation was that he had not confessed his feelings and utterly ruined their friendship. In light of all he had hoped might exist between them, it was not much comfort.

He did not want to hear anymore and, for the first time, wanted to be away from Fenbridge's company. "It looks as if it might rain. Shall we head back?"

"Er, yes. If you wish."

They packed up the remains of the meal and got their reluctant horses moving, Benjamin leading the way back to Edinburgh, the only thought in his mind being a bottle of whiskey and subsequent oblivion.

CHAPTER FOURTEEN

LOTTIE STARED up at the building - more of a castle than a house - in front of her. It was several times larger than the small country estate her own family owned. She had not realised before how rich Mr Alexander Fenbridge was and her former nerves returned: could he really be content to make her the mistress of so grand a building and put her in charge of those who ran it.

The servants were all in attendance to greet Mr Fenbridge, lined up in rows that presumably represented the different household and outdoor departments - housekeeper; maids, butler, footmen, cooks, grooms, gardeners... There must be a hundred people.

Having walked round the carriage to her side, Mr Fenbridge took her arm and, with a smile, led her forward and introduced her to the most senior of the various servants. He spoke to them in an affectionate manner which she could see they returned and they greeted her with bows or curtsies and polite smiles. A few of the others looked at her with open curiosity.

Mr Fenbridge then led Lottie and her parents into the house, which was every bit as grand and elegant as its exterior suggested, from the tapestries on the walls to the sweeping staircase ahead of them. The hall tables and grandfather clock gleamed as if they had just been polished.

"Would you care for a tour," Mr Fenbridge asked her, "or would you like to rest for a while before dinner?"

"A tour of the house would be lovely," she said, trying not to sound utterly intimidated by her surroundings.

Her father asked to be shown his room - he looked worn out from the long journey - but her mother accompanied them, no doubt feeling that a chaperon was still needed. As Mr Fenbridge led them round the ground floor he gave a brief history of the building and its more interesting features, adding, "Naturally you will be at liberty to change anything you do not like."

"Oh, no," she said at once. "It is beautiful."

"It is an elegant place but I know that some of the décor is old-fashioned. This is your home now and I want you to be happy here."

With this, her worries eased and she remembered why she had been so glad to accept his proposal.

"I hope we will both be happy," she said, determined to do her best to ensure it.

He gave her a warm smile and agreed.

* * *

Amelia was distracting herself from her life. She refused to think about Mr Wrackley - he was gone for good so it was pointless to pine for him. She would have to see Mr Brightford at some point, but she had no idea how she felt about him at the moment. It hurt to think his opinion of her was so low and she could not yet work out whether that view was justified or not or whether he had had the right to speak of it to Mr Wrackley. She felt too bereft at losing Lottie and Mr Wrackley's departure to be able to consider Mr Brightford so she was putting that from her mind too. She was beginning to get a headache from all the things she was not thinking about.

She spent half of the next morning looking through her clothes to decide what to take to Lottie and Mr Alexander Fenbridge's wedding. It did not matter that she was not leaving for two months; planning the trip made her feel better. Several gowns and bonnets were not bright enough for her liking so she took her maid to the shops to purchase ribbon to improve them. When she got back to the house she could almost believe that she felt perfectly content.

The footman handed her out of the carriage and she walked into her home, pausing in the hallway when she heard her mother's normally calm voice, high-pitched and distraught. Heart thudding painfully in her chest, she walked towards the library just as the butler ran out of the room.

She caught his arm. "Stewart, what is wrong?"

"Forgive me, Miss," he said, pulling away and hurrying towards the servants' stairs, "I must fetch the doctor at once."

She kept moving towards the library and put a hand on the intricately carved oak door, pushing it further open. Her father was lying on the floor, clutching his chest, her Mama kneeling beside him.

"No!" Amelia ran forward and sank to the floor, taking her father's hand.

His face was a terrible grey colour. His eyes slowly moved to Amelia's face and he mouthed her name then he wrenched his hand from hers, clutching his chest one final time.

His body jerked then went limp and, as she watched helplessly, his eyes emptied of life.

* * *

Mr Alexander Fenbridge had arranged for Josie Smith, one of the household maids, to act as Lottie's personal maid since her own maid had family in Edinburgh and did not wish to leave. Smith was a middle-aged woman who had seen Mr Fenbridge's sisters grow up in the house - her list of their accomplishments was never-ending.

"You should invite them to dine here," Lottie's mother insisted.

"How can I?" she asked. "I am not the mistress here."

"You soon will be and you need them to see that their brother is marrying the sort of lady they would wish him to wed: someone who can run his household flawlessly; organise and act as hostess for countless balls, dinner parties, etc. They are important ladies of the area, respected here and in their visits to the city. Their support could do you a great deal of good but if you fail to make a good impression..." She let her sentence tail off, her expression leaving no doubt that Lottie must do this and do it perfectly.

She reluctantly mentioned the idea to Mr Fenbridge later that day and he agreed at once, saying that an informal dinner party would be an excellent way for her and his sisters to become friends. Her spirits lifted by his confidence, she wrote out the invitations and gave them to the butler for delivery, letting him know that the dinner would be in two days' time. His stony expression immediately made her worry that she had done something wrong: perhaps the invitations were too formal or maybe he did not feel the household was being enough notice to arrange everything. She ventured to suggest that she could alter the date, which he seemed to take as a criticism, telling her stiffly that this was unnecessary and the staff were perfectly capable of fulfilling any duty she had for them.

By the time the cook came into the drawing room to discuss the menu with her, Lottie's courage was failing her. She was sure that the cook meant her suggestions kindly but she was left feeling that she could get nothing right.

Mr Alexander Fenbridge should have asked Amelia to marry him, Lottie thought despairingly. Amelia had all the confidence, determination and leadership abilities to take control of staff and home and to win the admiration of all her neighbours. Amelia was everything Lottie was not.

CHAPTER FIFTEEN

AMELIA WOKE hoping the previous day had been a nightmare - it did not seem possible that her father was suddenly gone - but the silenced clocks and black drapes around the pictures told her otherwise. The dining room, laid out for breakfast, was empty and she went in search of her mother, finding her in her father's study.

Mrs Daventry was in a chair at the desk frowning at a handful of papers. Without looking up she said, "People will want payment for bills. Your father would expect me to handle this but I do not know what to do."

Amelia pulled another chair up to the desk. "Then we will do it together."

Her resolve quickly faded to fear. Neither of them could make sense of the various receipts and bills - did the money need to be paid or had it already been paid? How much money did they have and where was it invested? Mr Daventry had been in charge of all such matters and had never mentioned the subject to either of them. Surely only men understood such things? Yet sometimes a woman inherited an estate from her father or husband so there must be some way of getting it to make sense.

They eventually gave up, defeated, and Mrs Daventry

said she would make an appointment with the family man of business who would hopefully be able to explain to them what money they had and what to do about expenses and bills.

Amelia set about writing a notice to go in the Edinburgh Gazette stating where and when the funeral would be held and there were a few distant relatives who would also need to be informed.

The breakfast in the dining room remained uneaten.

* * *

"I believe I expressed myself badly when we last spoke," Mr Nathaniel Fenbridge said as they played a game of billiards in Benjamin's home. "When I mentioned nearly getting engaged, what I meant was that as easy as it would have been to do as everyone expected, I would have been unfair to myself and to the lady in question if I had. Sometimes one's heart leads in a different direction."

Benjamin tried to take this in. The words seemed a confirmation of his own feelings but he had been wrong so many times it did not seem possible and, after the picnic, his hopes had been destroyed entirely.

Fenbridge continued, "May I ask why you were concerned about your future?"

"My father wishes me to marry."

Fenbridge stared at him. He seemed taken aback by this announcement but otherwise Benjamin could not read his emotions. "Who?"

"Someone of good family, the wealthier the better. Other than that, anyone would do."

"What do you want?"

This was the moment; the choice between two paths. Should he tell Fenbridge of his feelings or should he lie and say he was perfectly amenable to the idea of marriage? He opened his mouth, still with no idea what to do, and the words came out of their own volition: "I do not ever wish to marry."

Fenbridge gave a shaky smile and put a hand on his shoulder, squeezing it lightly. "Then I think you should not."

"My father might disinherit me."

"I am quite certain that, if it becomes necessary, my brother would let you live on his estate."

Benjamin swallowed, his heart beating so loudly he wondered if Fenbridge could hear it. "Why would he do that?"

"To make me happy. *You* make me happy."

Benjamin leaned closer. "As you do. I mean, you also make me…"

Fenbridge kissed him and every problem vanished. It was Benjamin's first kiss and the sensation of Fenbridge's warm lips against his was a revelation. He held on to the other man as every seemingly insurmountable obstacle between them vanished.

* * *

The funeral was like a bad dream to Amelia. She tried to hold back the tears but it was as if she was only realising now that her father truly was gone. Out of both her parents, he had always been the more indulgent one; the one who could understand her point of view and rarely criticised her. She would miss him so much.

She could not have said whether it was sunny or raining in the churchyard. A blackness seemed to surround her and no warmth or brightness penetrated it.

Guests came back to the house after the funeral and she accepted their condolences numbly, wishing with all her heart for Lottie, who would have made this bearable.

She saw Mr Brightford talking to people and could not even find the energy to be angry with him. His presence just added to her grief.

"Have you eaten yet today?" Benjamin asked her, Mr Nathaniel Fenbridge at his side. She had not even seen them approach.

Had she eaten? She tried to remember. "I do not think so."

"Then you must have something."

"I will fetch it." Mr Nathaniel touched her arm, expression full of sympathy, then he walked away towards the table that had been laid out with food.

"He is a good man," she said, glad to have something to distract her mind. "Did you tell him what your father said?"

"Yes." He smiled.

"You will not be marrying?"

The smile widened and his eyes followed Mr Fenbridge's movements with clear affection. "No, I will not marry."

"Good."

She sat with them and ate some food, although it seemed tasteless and indigestible. Other people began to drift away. Mr Brightford caught her eyes, looking as if he wanted to say something, before he turned and left.

"We will gladly stay for a while if you and your mother do not wish to be alone," Benjamin said.

"I do not think either of us is capable of sensible conversation today," she said. "I think we need some time on our own to grieve."

The house felt particularly empty after they left and Amelia gave in to the need to cry unreservedly.

CHAPTER SIXTEEN

AMELIA AND HER mother spent two hours the next morning in a confusing meeting with the family man of business. Amelia had suggested that it wait a few days but Mama had wanted to get it out of the way. Mr Brodie had made it clear their situation was bad but had rattled through so many things they did not understand – what were the funds? which bank had collapsed? - that they came out of the office with no better understanding of their finances than when they had entered. If Amelia's head had been clearer she would have demanded him to explain himself clearly but, as it was, his constant references to her father just deepened her grief and she could not give the matter the attention it warranted; indeed, she just wanted to escape.

The law building was in the centre of the New Town and, upon leaving, they ran into the last person in the world Amelia wanted to see. He bowed to them and she responded with a brief curtsy.

"My deepest condolences to you both," Mr Brightford said, his frown one of sympathy not disapproval for once, but no more welcome than usual. "I did not want to disturb you at the funeral but I wanted you to know that I liked and respected Mr Daventry a great deal. Everyone did."

She bit her lip to stop herself commenting on how little he liked her, unable to cope with him today, while her mother gave a polite response.

As they turned away he added, "Let me know if there is anything I can do."

This was too much and she glared at him over her shoulder: "Do you not think you have done more than enough?"

She saw his start of surprise at this and then a distinctly guilty expression.

She followed her mother to their carriage and climbed in.

"What was it you said to Mr Brightford?" Mrs Daventry asked her as she smoothed down her black mourning dress.

Amelia shook her head and then, out of the blue, started to sob.

* * *

Benjamin called on Mrs Daventry and Amelia mid-afternoon to see how they were getting on. Mr Daventry had been a kind, friendly man - indeed, Benjamin had often wished his own father could have been more like him.

He found them in the drawing room, both subdued while Amelia's eyes were red from crying and his heart went out to them both. He could not even imagine their pain.

They had not needed his help with the funeral arrangements but there surely must be something he could do for them now: "Tell me what you need done. Letters? Perhaps packing away some of Mr Daventry's possessions?"

"It is extremely kind of you…" Mrs Daventry began.

"Do you know anything of financial papers?" Amelia cut in.

"Amelia, you cannot ask such a thing," her mother scolded.

"No, please, let me help," Benjamin insisted. "Tell me what you need explained and I will endeavour to do so. If there is anything that is unclear to me - and there might well be as my father handles a lot of our affairs - I will fetch Mr Nathaniel Fenbridge to go through it with you."

"We could not impose on you or Mr Fenbridge like that," Mrs Daventry said.

"I have always had the very highest opinion of Mr Daventry and Amelia has been a second sister to me. I sincerely wish to help."

Mrs Daventry hesitated then nodded, clearly embarrassed at needing assistance. "Then I thank you. If you can make more sense than our solicitor did we will be eternally grateful to you."

Several hours later they had gone through all the papers, the task of which bills still needed to be paid much easier once they came across the accounts book Mr Daventry had kept. Both women understood his explanations quickly, although they seemed surprised to be able to do so.

He had known that the family was not a wealthy one but the situation was worse than he had expected. If Amelia did not marry a rich man they might well have to sell their estate and, although that would leave them enough money for comfortable lives, it would leave nothing for any future generations.

They both offered him grateful smiles and thanked him for his help but Benjamin remained concerned for them.

* * *

Mr Alexander Fenbridge's sisters arrived with their respective husbands at exactly the correct time for the dinner party and were shown into the drawing room where Mr Fenbridge introduced them to Lottie. The elder sister – Mrs Henrietta Stanton - had light brown hair while the younger woman – Mrs Catherine Wentford - was blonde, but other than this their looks were similar: regal and aloof in a way that magnified Lottie's nervousness. After all her mother's comments on the subject Lottie felt as if her entire future marriage depended on tonight being perfect.

She had invited a few extra people to increase the numbers and, as a friend of the family, had been forced to include Mr Wrackley. She disliked him for causing Amelia pain and had no desire to spend any time in his company, so she excused herself as soon as she had greeted him. The guests made small talk while awaiting the final people and Lottie silently went over the order of precedence for the procession to the dining room, desperately hoping she had got it correct and no one would be offended. When everyone was assembled and the butler had announced the meal Mr Fenbridge led his elder sister into the dining room with the rest of the gentlemen taking the ladies' arms and following, in strict rank order. Lottie, as an unmarried woman, was last, led in by the loquacious parish priest, who distracted her briefly from her nerves.

Everyone took their assigned seats, the giant epergne in the middle of the table providing most of the light while, unfortunately, blocking Mr Fenbridge and his elder sister from her sight. Mrs Wentford, his younger sister, was to Lottie's right, after Mr Smithton, the priest. Aware that half the purpose of the meal was for her to become acquainted with the rest of Mr Fenbridge's family, Lottie tried to get in some conversation with Mrs Wentford but was largely thwarted by Mr Smithton's inability to stop speaking.

Four courses into the meal – about halfway through – she managed to knock over her glass of red wine. She stared at it in horror as one of the footmen hastened forward to clear up the mess.

"Really, Charlotte, you can be so clumsy," her mother scolded in a loud voice, so that everyone at the table must be aware of Lottie's failure.

From that moment onwards she could do nothing right. The blush never left her cheeks; she was tongue-tied and, when she could speak, she stammered over her words.

By the end of the night, when the guests had departed, she was so mortified so could not look Mr Fenbridge in the eye. How heartily he must regret having picked such a fool to marry.

CHAPTER SEVENTEEN

"DID YOU TELL Miss Daventry what I said about her to Wrackley?"

It was two days after Mr Daventry's funeral and Mr Brightford was feeling sorry for the family and wretched over spoiling Miss Daventry's chance at a good marriage. He tried to tell himself that Wrackley would have been miserable to discover after marriage that Miss Daventry had only ever wanted his money and not him, but he was no longer sure about any of this. He could not forget the look of distress and anger on her face when he encountered her yesterday.

"Yes, I did," Fenbridge admitted, putting down a cup of coffee. "I will not apologise for it. I like Miss Daventry and I think you have treated her extremely ill."

Brightford could not be annoyed with him when he knew Fenbridge had acted out of his usual kindness. "Perhaps you are right. I felt I had a duty to tell Wrackley the truth but now I am not so sure, particularly in light of what she is currently suffering."

"More than you know."

Brightford made a look of enquiry. "How so?"

"I reveal this only in the strictest confidence but Benj-

Harrington helped the family understand their finances and I gather the situation is dire."

"That was why she needed Wrackley's money."

Fenbridge frowned. "I believe she loved him. I am not certain she was even aware of his wealth. I certainly never mentioned it and, while you were in my presence, which you usually were around Miss Daventry, I do not believe you or my brother ever mentioned it."

Brightford frowned over this idea. If it was true then his interference had been unconscionable. Mr Daventry had asked him of Mr Wrackley's character but, no, the subject of wealth had never been mentioned and he had never spoken of it to Miss Daventry. "In the past I had overheard her speaking of getting herself a rich, powerful husband."

"Given her family's situation it doubtless seemed like something she must consider but, when it came to it, I believe her heart led her to Wrackley."

"Then I have harmed her in a way I do not have any idea how to fix." He would have to try. His conscience demanded it.

* * *

Lottie was arranging roses from the garden into a vase the morning after her disastrous dinner party. Mr Alexander Fenbridge had made no criticisms of her so far today but she dreaded the thought that he might not wish to marry her any more. He had chosen her to be an accomplished hostess and manage his home capably and she had failed her first self-appointed task. She was deep in these thoughts when the footman came in.

"Mrs Wentford to see you, Miss Harrington."

He had barely finished speaking when Mr Fenbridge's younger sister swept into the dining room, flawlessly lovely despite the heat of the day, in lavender satin. Lottie, feeling a dowdy mess in comparison, curtsied and sent the butler for lemonade while they sat down.

"I wanted to apologise to you and Mrs Stanton for making such a mess of the dinner party last night."

Mrs Wentford raised an elegant eyebrow. "Did you make a mess?"

"I spilt my wine."

Mrs Wentford laughed. "My sister and I are hardly so fussy that we would condemn you for so tiny a thing, but it is flattering to my brother and us that you were so concerned that the evening be perfect."

"I truly did and then I ended up clumsy and tongue-tied."

"You are too critical of yourself. My brother thinks highly of you which is all that is really important."

"Does he?" Without intending to she found herself blurting out her greatest fear. "I keep fearing he will change his mind."

"He is not the capricious type. He loves you."

"Oh, no. It was not a romantic proposal. Mr Fenbridge believed I would make him a practical wife."

"Oh, dear." Mrs Wentworth gave a dimpled smile. "I think Alex must have been too nervous to confess his feelings to you but, as someone who knows him well, I can assure you he cares deeply for you. He will certainly think nothing of the occasional spilt drink."

Lottie laughed, relieved and pleased by these words and by Mrs Wentford's support. After a couple of hours talking she considered Mrs Wentford a friend, the lady displaying the same friendliness and kind nature as her brothers, along with a lively interest in all that went on in the parish. By the time she left Lottie had learnt a great deal about her new home and felt more relaxed than she had since arriving.

As she went for a walk in the garden, she considered what Mrs Wentford had said about Mr Fenbridge. Lottie had not thought she would ever have love in her life again

- had not believed she could trust it - but it gave her a burst of happiness to think that Mr Fenbridge had deeper feelings for her than she had known.

* * *

A week went by and then two. Amelia thought little of what was happening in the outside world. She knew, with a kind of dazed disbelief, that the season was drawing to a close, that people were still attending card parties, balls and dinner parties, but it seemed impossible to her that there could still be pleasure in the world when her own life and that of her mother were so bleak.

Her grief still befuddled her senses so the interview she and mama had had with their man of business yesterday had been particularly difficult. They must sell their estate in order to have enough money to live, he had told them. Mama had refused. Amelia had no idea what was for the best, although it hurt to think of giving up the family home Papa had worked all his life to keep.

The butler announced Mr Benjamin Harrington and she automatically got to her feet and curtsied to him as he bowed. She put down the cushion cover she had been staring at - it should have been a gift for her father but she had embroidered too slowly, easily distracted by trivial pleasures, and he had never seen it. She knew he had loved her but had she ever done anything to make him proud of her?

Mr Harrington held out a letter which she accepted. "It is from Lottie," he said. "I wrote to tell her immediately of your father's death."

She gave a watery smile, the piece of paper immediately priceless to her. "Thank you."

"How are you today? Was it yesterday you were going back to the solicitor?"

"Unfortunately, yes." They sat down and she told him

as much as she could remember of what had been said. "Do you think there is anything we can do to save the estate?"

"I believe your father managed to raise enough money for your family to live on through careful investments. It would make sense to continue doing the same."

"I know nothing of such things. Could you advise me?"

"I fear I know as little as you but I will ask Fenbridge and Brightford."

"Not Mr Brightford," she said quickly. "He has a low opinion of me and I think it best to have as little to do with him from now on as possible."

He stiffened at this. "What has happened?"

"It is not important. He is now brother-in-law to you and Lottie and I know he is your friend. Let me simply say that we have had a disagreement."

"Let us not," he exclaimed, frowning. "For him to upset you when you are grieving…"

"He did not," she reassured him and wished she had never brought up the man. "I thought myself in love with Mr Wrackley when he was here and he… he seemed to care for me. Mr Brightford said some things to him that, I believe, caused him to change his opinion of me and leave."

"What did he say?"

She bit her lip. "That I was interested in nothing but Mr Wrackley's money. It is not true…"

"Of course it is not," he said angrily. "How dare he behave so?"

"I suppose he believed it to be true. In the past I have thought how nice it would be to be rich."

"So do a lot of people. I have no doubt Lottie dreamed of riches on occasion and I have certainly wished for more money to spend on our estate."

"But Lottie was the romantic one…"

"And now she has made a thoroughly sensible match. I sincerely hope she will grow to love Mr Alexander

Fenbridge but she is certainly not infatuated at present and I would fight any man who criticised her for it. She did what she thought was best for her and that is what you will do and I hope you will have the luxury of finding your heart and good sense lead you to a man of good character and reasonable wealth."

"Mr Wrackley had both, although I did not know it nor, at the time, care about his finances." It seemed so long ago, a bright, happy time long gone, replaced by long difficult days and constant sadness.

"Brightford should be horse-whipped."

Amelia grabbed his arm, alarmed by his anger. "Benjamin, promise me you will not challenge him to a duel."

"I should…"

"No. I want you to do nothing about this. You must give me your word. If I was responsible for either you or Mr Brightford dying I do not know how I would live with it. At the time he thought he was acting for the best and perhaps his words made no difference at all: if Mr Wrackley had truly loved me could he have been so easily put off? Promise me you will not challenge him."

He gave a curt nod. "Very well."

When he took his leave Amelia sat down and, once she had managed to convince herself no one was going to die in a duel, she calmed and opened Lottie's letter.

* * *

"I should challenge you to a duel but Miss Daventry made me promise not to."

Mr Brightford, sitting in his study getting very little done, regarded the glaring figure of Harrington with a jaundiced eye. It had been a long morning and he was not in the mood to cope with hot-headed youths. "Then I suppose I must be grateful to Miss Daventry."

"She can hardly say the same, can she? I got her to tell me what you said to Mr Wrackley." His anger dimmed into a confused disappointment that was somehow more galling: "How could you do such a thing?"

"I misjudged her and, I promise you, I have already been taken to task over it by Nathan. If I could take back my words I would. I have been trying to think of a way to make amends but thus far can think of nothing."

"There is a way but since Amelia specifically said she did not wish for your advice, you will have to keep thinking." He began to walk out but turned when Brightford called after him.

"I do heartily regret my words."

Benjamin nodded. "Did it never occur to you that, like you, there is far more to Miss Daventry than can easily be ascertained at a ball or other diversion. She is intelligent and kind but those are sides of her that are not seen unless one takes the time to get to know her."

He left Brightford to ponder these words.

* * *

Lottie's affectionate letter had left Amelia feeling more lonely than ever but she now thought of the upcoming visit and wedding with more interest than she had felt in anything since her father's death.

Of course, the hateful Mr Brightford would be attending the wedding too but she could not avoid him forever and why should she? She was not the one in the wrong. And yet what had given him the idea she might be interested in Mr Wrackley for his money? It was not true but she had thought of men in mercenary terms in the past. She had told herself she was being practical but had she instead been callous or greedy? Yet Benjamin had understood and not condemned her.

She did not know what to think, except that Mr

Brightford had now beaten Mr Saverney as the most unpleasant man she had ever met.

CHAPTER EIGHTEEN

"MADAM, I BELIEVE I owe you an apology."

Her mother was out visiting friends so Amelia had reluctantly agreed to speak to Mr Brightford when he called at the house. She could have refused him since it was not proper for her to see him without a chaperone – she had already waived this rule for Benjamin and Mr Nathaniel Fenbridge but that was because she wanted to. She considered sending him away but curiosity got the better of her so she joined him in the drawing room.

His tone was uncomfortable as he made his apology and she wondered if he actually meant it or had been persuaded to say this by his friends. She sat down and he did the same. "You *believe*, sir? You have doubts then?"

"No. I do owe you an apology and my sincere regrets for what I said about you to Mr Wrackley."

"Because it was ungentlemanly or because it was untrue?"

"Both."

She frowned, surprised by this capitulation and wondering what Benjamin had said to him to bring it about. "You have had an extremely sudden change of heart about my character then?"

"Yes… I mean, not exactly. I think part of my initial concerns were reasonable but… no, I do not mean that…"

"I am at a loss to understand what you do mean," she said, anger rising. "You apparently believed me to be a heartless mercenary only interested in money."

"Well, I had heard you talk about money before…"

Loathsome man! This was his idea of an apology? "Is it a sin to speak of money?"

"I thought it unladylike but that is not the point…"

"On the contrary, I am fascinated to learn how you came to feel you were an expert judge on perfection of character. Are you without flaw of any kind?"

"No, not at all."

"Then what right did you have to ruin my future happiness and make up your mind I was some evil person?"

"None at all. I apologise…"

She slapped him as hard as she could, the sound loud in the sudden silence. Her hand immediately stung and after a moment she realised what she had done. She stared at Mr Brightford in horror then turned and fled.

* * *

Brightford watched Amelia run up the stairs then heard the sound of a door banging shut.

His face was sore where she had slapped him but he wanted to tell her he did not blame her for the action. What an utter mess he had made of that apology. She had deserved his deepest regret over what he had done, not his censure for matters which she was right in saying he had no business to judge.

He had come here with every intention of offering his abject regrets over his words but somehow it had all gone wrong. He walked into the hallway where the butler handed him his hat and cane with a look that said *good riddance*.

He felt thoroughly uncomfortable as he headed out to his curricle. Miss Daventry was an argumentative woman, surely that could not be denied. She had seemed determined to quarrel… or perhaps she had just doubted his sincerity, which again he could not fault her on.

He wondered if his cheek was red from the blow she had landed. She had certainly put her full force behind it.

He drove around the nearby park, not acknowledging that he wanted some extra time before facing Nathan with the confession of how utterly he had botched the visit. If he was unlucky Harrington would be there too, both of them keen to tell him what an idiot he was.

As he finally headed home, there was one thing he was certain of: Miss Daventry brought out the worst in him and their trip together to his cousin's wedding was going to be a nightmare…

* * *

Amelia sat on the chair in her bedroom and stared blankly at the wallpaper opposite her. She could not believe she had slapped Mr Brightford. While he had certainly provoked her with his critical, half-hearted apology, nothing could justify her reaction. Now she owed him an apology but that would meant raising the subject and she felt humiliated just thinking of it. What was even worse was that she had now justified his low opinion of her character.

She was only half aware of the sound of a carriage pulling up somewhere outside, not paying it any attention until several minutes later when there was a loud knock upon their front door.

She walked downstairs as the butler admitted a middle-aged but beautifully dressed lady to the house. She was tall and dark-haired with the air of someone who knew her own importance. Mrs Daventry crossed the hall to greet the stranger as Amelia got to the bottom of the stairs.

"You wrote to inform me of my brother's death," the woman said in a loud voice, in answer to Mrs Daventry's enquiry about her visit. "I am Mrs Gallerton."

Papa's estranged sister. The one he had not spoken to since before Amelia had been born.

"It is kind of you to call on us..." Mrs Daventry began.

"Nonsense," Mrs Gallerton cut over her. "I should have come when Richard was still alive but there is nothing to be done about that now and at least I can get to know you and your daughter." Her sharp eyes took in Amelia in her black dress and she beckoned her forward. "Come here, young lady, and tell me your name."

Amelia did as she was told, amused that she seemed to have a relation even more forthright and opinionated than herself.

CHAPTER NINETEEN

AFTER FIVE DAYS of Mrs Gallerton's company Amelia was no longer amused; in fact she was close to screaming.

Mrs Gallerton expressed her opinions on every subject, frequently telling them ways they could improve their home or get more work out of the servants and clearly expecting them to immediately jump to obey her. Of course, neither Mama nor herself had done any such thing, leading to some tense moments.

In other circumstances Amelia might have shaken it off and found her aunt interesting, but neither Mama nor herself were at their best right now and Mrs Gallerton seemed intent on making their lives more difficult instead of easier.

While the three of them were in the dining room for afternoon tea, Amelia brought up the subject of Lottie's wedding to her mother. She had been worried about doing so, uncertain as to whether her mother would want the long journey or consider the wedding too frivolous an event to attend while they were in mourning. As it turned out she need not have been concerned.

"Yes, of course we will attend," Mrs Daventry said as she lifted a piece of buttered scone to her lips. "Charlotte is your best friend and Mr and Mrs Harrington are friends of mine and your father… are friends of mine."

"A change of air will lift both your spirits," Mrs Gallerton contributed, "and England is far warmer than this. I am used to proper summers. I will join you."

Amelia and her mother exchanged glances. The woman might at least wait to be asked.

Mrs Daventry took another sip of tea. "I will ask Mr Benjamin Harrington when he wishes to leave."

The next day, when Benjamin called to check on them, they agreed a date two weeks' hence to set out and he also, on Lottie's behalf, invited Amelia's aunt to join them. Depending on how many days the journey took that would give them about three weeks at Mr Alexander Fenbridge's home before the wedding.

Amelia could not wait, the need to see her friend suddenly overwhelming. Lottie's letter had also made Amelia miss her all the more and the knowledge that Lottie would never again live within a short carriage ride's distance made it even worse, so she intended to make the most of every moment of their visit.

There was not much to get ready for the journey and she and her mother would, of course, still be wearing their black mourning outfits so there would not be anything to decide over clothes, despite her aunt's comments to the contrary.

The days crawled by with little for Amelia to occupy herself with save worrying about the family finances, fretting over her future and feeling mortified over slapping Mr Brightford. She had not seen him since the awful incident but knew from Benjamin that he would be amongst the party travelling to the wedding.

She believed herself to have a generally happy disposition but her father's death and not having Lottie here to help her cope with it made everything seem almost unbearable. Also, for some reason, the fact that Mr Brightford had such a poor opinion of her kept preying on her mind. She realised with a start that she had thought far more about that than about losing Mr Wrackley's regard. Did she simply not have any grief left to spare him or was it possible that she had not loved him after all?

* * *

"You must be looking forward to seeing your family again for your sister's wedding," Mr Nathaniel Fenbridge said to Benjamin as they sat having luncheon together, "or are you worried about not obeying your father's decree to get engaged?"

"I will be very happy to see Lottie but I fear my parents will cut me out of their lives when I tell them I never intend to marry." It was an encounter he was dreading but he told himself they could only disown him once so, once it was done, he could forget about it and enjoy seeing Lottie again. It galled him that he would be dependent on Nathan to support him, that it might put a strain on their relationship, but Nathan had reassured him a number of times on the subject. Also, Benjamin hoped to throw himself into assisting with the running of Alexander Fenbridge's estate and perhaps be sufficiently useful to make up for the financial assistance.

He would have to find a way to make it work as he knew he could never give Nathan up. Their weeks together had given him a joy he hadn't previously known was possible, the mutual affection and physical intimacies giving him everything he could ever want.

Nathan took his hand, pulling his thoughts back to the present. "If you wanted to give them extra time to get used to us you could always say you are not marrying for the moment."

"No. They have had a couple of years to get used to my feelings and their solution is to force me to live as others do even if it makes me miserable. If they cannot cope with who I am then I am resigned to being disowned. You make me happy and that is all I need from life."

They exchanged a kiss and Nathan said, "Then I will endeavour to always make you happy."

* * *

Miss Daventry had been on Mr Brightford's mind recently.

Harrington - in reaction to hearing about Brightford's words to Wrackley - had insisted on telling him countless stories about Miss Daventry's kindness, wittiness and affectionate nature. Then, when he had run out of breath, Fenbridge took over. Had the annoying woman set out to charm every man she had ever met save him?

No, she had doubtless never intended it but the stories had done their work and Brightford had begun to be won over as well. Just this morning he had had to reprimand himself for dwelling on how beautiful she was and wishing she did not dislike him so thoroughly.

The knowledge that she was not the person he had believed made the harm he had done her all the more grievous and he could think of only one way to make amends.

He sat down at his writing desk and began the difficult task of composing a letter to Mr Wrackley.

CHAPTER TWENTY

ON THE DAY they were due to leave for Mr Alexander Fenbridge's estate Amelia was packed and ready by 7am, her Mama was ready by 9am, the carriage with the rest of the party was there by 9.30am and Aunt Agnes was still procrastinating at midday.

"We should have luncheon then leave," Mrs Gallerton announced to the group assembled in the drawing room.

"We have a picnic packed for luncheon," Amelia reminded her as patiently as she was able.

"I wish I had been introduced to either the bride or groom." She said this in the tone of one who has been ill-treated. "It does not feel entirely proper to be expected to stay with complete strangers."

Amelia bit her tongue to prevent herself from pointing out that this unexpected sensitivity had not stopped her aunt turning up on their doorstep.

"My brother will be delighted to have you stay with him," Mr Nathaniel Fenbridge reassured her with his usual good humour.

"Or if you really feel you would rather stay here until we return you are welcome to do so," Amelia suggested in a tone that must have sounded too hopeful from the glare her mother shot at her and the cool look from her aunt.

"Thank you, Mr Fenbridge. I will accept your word for it. I just need to check I have everything I need then I suppose we should set off." She vanished back out of the room.

Amelia sighed and Benjamin suggested a game of cards.

* * *

Half an hour after they finally departed Amelia would have given anything to be back in her room.

Mrs Gallerton had invited Mr Brightford to join their carriage. Indeed she looked as if she would have liked to join all three gentlemen but sadly lacked the level of audacity needed to invite herself into their carriage. This meant that Amelia now shared a carriage with her mother, Mrs Gallerton and Mr Brightford while Benjamin and Mr Nathaniel Fenbridge shared the other. The latter gentlemen looked more than satisfied at the arrangement while Amelia resolved herself to two days of misery and humiliation.

While Mrs Gallerton talked at everyone on any subject that entered her head, Amelia tried to avoid Mr Brightford's gaze, which meant she spent most of her time looking out of the window.

"You are in a quiet mood, Amelia," Mrs Gallerton said and Amelia started and looked round. "Normally you have far more to say for yourself and Mrs Daventry and I have heard all this last week how eager you are to see your friend." Before Amelia could respond, Mrs Gallerton turned to Mr Brightford and added, "It is pleasant for a young lady to attend a wedding, although of course not nearly as pleasant as her own wedding." She laughed at her own slight joke while Mr Brightford gave an uncomfortable smile - more of a grimace really - and Amelia felt her face heat. "I imagine you are thinking about marriage yourself, Mr Brightford," Mrs Gallerton went on with such an utter lack of subtlety that Amelia longed to throw herself from the carriage to escape.

"Not when I can avoid it," Mr Brightford replied and Amelia, for once, welcomed his lack of manners, hoping it would put her aunt off the subject.

"Of course, men have more leisure over these matters than women…"

Amelia wondered if she could enlist some help in pushing Mrs Gallerton from the carriage. From the expressions around her she suspected no one would object.

"I am glad today is cooler than it has been recently," Mrs Daventry said hastily and Amelia threw her mother a grateful look.

"Indeed," Mr Brightford agreed eagerly. "There is nothing worse than a stuffy carriage ride."

Not to be left out, Mrs Gallerton said, "England is, of course, warmer than Scotland."

"The countryside is, I believe, different to ours," Amelia said, no longer caring how long Mrs Gallerton spoke just so long as she stopped match-making.

"That is very true. Where I live…"

Amelia's wish was granted as her aunt managed to keep this subject going until they stopped at a large inn. It was only late afternoon but they agreed that this would be a good place to spend the night.

While her mother rested in the room they would be sharing, Amelia went for a short walk to clear her head of the echo of Mrs Gallerton's strident voice.

She wandered vaguely towards some trees, enjoying the weak sunshine and the cool breeze on her face. She was brought to a half by the sight of a familiar figure. Her instinct was to turn and flee but she ignored it and steeled herself to approach.

"Mr Brightford," she said to get his attention.

Her turned round, looking equally startled by her

presence, and bowed.

She curtsied. "Mr Brightford, I owe you an apology for my shameful behaviour in slapping you when we last spoke. I do not know what caused me to act in such a way."

"I expect it was my own appalling manners," he said easily. "Besides, I still owe you an apology over Mr Wrackley."

"You have already made it."

"But you did not accept it," he pointed out with a sardonic lift to one eyebrow.

She smiled, awkwardness fading. "Then I do so now and I hope you will likewise forgive me."

"Done."

Her relief at his response was beyond what it should have been and for a moment she remained flustered in his presence. "Mr Nathaniel Fenbridge must be looking forward to seeing his brother again," she ventured.

"One might suppose that but in actual fact I have never seen him more content than during these last weeks."

Her smile returned. "I believe he and Mr Harrington have formed an affectionate friendship."

He gave her a sharp look and his eyes flashed with amusement. "That would seem to be a very accurate way of putting it."

Did he know? Mr Nathaniel Fenbridge was his relative so it was not impossible and it would greatly improve her opinion of him if he did not choose to condemn his cousin.

"Then I am very glad for them both."

"As am I," he said.

It was the first time they had been in agreement about anything.

* * *

Mr Brightford changed into his evening clothes, a smile on his lips as he thought about his conversation with Miss Daventry. He had enjoyed it a great deal. Far too much, in fact.

The fact she had forgiven him for so serious a misdeed was a great relief and that combined with her wit had entirely won him over. How could he have failed to see all her positive qualities all this time? He was sure she knew the truth about the relationship between Fenbridge and Harrington too and wished them well, which showed a rare tolerance.

Perhaps he should have told her about writing to Wrackley but she would see him at the wedding so they could resume their courtship soon.

His heart twinged at the thought.

He made a note to give up selfless behaviour: it was clearly not good for his health.

CHAPTER TWENTY-ONE

AMELIA SMILED with pleasure at the sight of Mr Alexander Fenbridge's estate, which would soon officially be Lottie's too, happy to finally get here and be on the verge of seeing her friend again.

The rest of the journey had passed much like the first day with slight variations of who travelled in which carriage and where they stopped to rest each night, Mrs Gallerton's non-stop chatter and hints about Amelia marrying constantly in her ears. After three days of this torture they finally reached their destination.

The countryside was beautiful, some of it farmland with men working in fields of wheat and vegetables, but closer to the estate was a large wooded area then a large fenced-off field with a few horses in and a long road leading up to the house. In front of the building was a circular garden with flowers and a waterfall. As Amelia got out of her carriage and tried to stretch her aching back in a surreptitious manner she saw that Lottie and Mr Alexander Fenbridge were on the doorstep to greet the group, behind them an impressively large medieval building three storeys high with turrets on either end.

Greetings and introductions were made and, as the

others talked and headed in, Lottie and Amelia hugged each other.

"It is so good to finally see you," Amelia said, almost overwhelmed at having her friend back again when she had felt Lottie's absence so keenly over the last few weeks.

"And you. I was so sorry to hear about your father," Lottie responded as she pulled back and held Amelia's hands. "You must miss him very much."

"It has been difficult. I did not know at first how we would bear it."

"He was the best of men."

"I know I will always miss him but I hope it will grow easier in time to not have him here. Now it is a constant ache."

"I am sure it will get better." Lottie let go of her hands but put an arm round her as she led Amelia inside, the rest of the party having already progressed to a room downstairs, presumably the drawing room. "Let me show you your room so you can unpack and rest." She glanced back over her shoulder to the room holding the others, where a loud female voice could be heard. "I did now know you had an aunt."

Mrs Gallerton had insisted on introductions to the couple almost before she was out of the carriage and was no doubt now telling Mr Alexander Fenbridge her life story.

"My father, very sensibly as it turns out, would not speak to her. You will quickly understand why." She looked around as they ascended a long elegant staircase. "This estate is beautiful."

"I will give you the full tour later, I promise. The gardens behind the house are lovely too."

Amelia paused then said hesitantly, "And is everything as you expected with Mr Alexander Fenbridge?"

"You mean, have I changed my mind about the marriage? No, I am more happy about it than ever. Alex is a wonderful man."

Amelia could see the truth of this in her face and manner. Lottie was more relaxed than she had been in months and had a glow of contentment about her. "I am glad."

"You do not intend to try and talk me out of it?"

"That is the last thing I wish to do. That you are happy is my sole concern and I have had more than enough trouble with people interfering in my life." She thought of Mr Brightford but had not for some time felt her previous dislike of him. Indeed, she had increasingly enjoyed his company on the journey here.

"What do you mean?" Lottie asked her.

Amelia shook her head, the story too long and complicated to go into now. Besides, she found she did now want Lottie to think badly of Mr Brightford, which was ridiculous since Lottie had always had to defend him from Amelia's criticisms. Their lives had certainly changed these last few months.

* * *

"What plans has everyone made for the afternoon?" Mrs Gallerton asked.

Benjamin, who had had to put up with her company in the carriage this morning, thought that he would happily volunteer to do anything that she would hate and, therefore, not join in with.

"I was thinking of riding out to visit my old friend, Mr Wrackley," Nathan said. "Harrington, I hoped you might accompany me so I could show you more of the estate on the way?"

"Delighted, sir." Benjamin could have kissed him and, now he thought of it, that would certainly put Mrs Gallerton off his company. If things got too desperate, it was worth considering.

He paid little attention to the remainder of the

conversation - which would have been a great deal more interesting if Mrs Gallerton had said far less - but rose at once when Nathan did so. In all honesty, it was less Mrs Gallerton than his parents he was happy to escape. They had not had an opportunity to speak to him in private yet and he knew there was an unpleasant scene ahead - probably just the first of many - when they discovered he was not engaged.

He changed into riding clothes then met Nathan at the stables outside where a groom was saddling two horses for them. He and Nathan exchanged grins then he petted the horses, getting acquainted with them, until they were ready to leave.

"It is pleasant to be out in the fresh air," Nathan said as their horses trotted side by side over the grass.

"It is pleasant to be away from Mrs Gallerton," Benjamin countered with feeling.

Nathan's tone became more intimate. "It is pleasant to be alone together."

Benjamin shivered at the suggestive tone, recalling their previous night together. "It is indeed."

It took them less than half an hour to reach Wrackley's estate, which was an even more impressive size than that of Mr Alexander Fenbridge.

"He is the wealthiest man in the county," Nathan revealed, "although he does not boast of it nor put on grand airs."

They handed over their horses to the groom of a large stable. Apparently Wrackley bred horses as a hobby and included several thoroughbreds among them, which Benjamin looked forward to discussing with him. It turned out not to be possible during this meeting, however.

"Did Miss Daventry come with you? Do you think I should go and speak to her at once?" Wrackley said the moment they had greeted each other, his handsome face animated and his mood restless.

"You had a change of heart over spurning her?"

Nathan guessed.

"Mr Brightford wrote to tell me he had been utterly wrong about her character and that he was sure she had been in love with me."

That fool. Benjamin listened in disbelief. Brightford and Amelia could have been engaged before Mr Alexander Fenbridge and Lottie were even married and now look at the mess Brightford had made of everything.

* * *

"There is something I must confess to you," Lottie said as they wandered through the estate's formal back garden which was full of a myriad of scents and colours. "Mr Wrackley has visited us since we have been back."

Amelia waited for a burst of unhappiness at the reminder of him and when it failed to appear she said, "That is hardly surprising since he and Mr Alexander Fenbridge are friends."

"No, but I thought of asking him why he had treated you the way he did and Alex convinced me not to. He had good reasons," she added hastily as if she expected a furious reaction from Amelia. "He thought that it might make things worse for you if we interfered and, in any case, Mr Wrackley will be at the wedding so he thought that that would be a better time to re-introduce you as a good friend of both of ours. What do you think?"

"There is something you do not know about." Amelia told her what Mr Brightford had said to Mr Wrackley and Lottie gave a gasp of outraged shock. "How could he be so cruel and unfair?"

"To be fair he had overheard me say in the past that I wanted a wealthy husband." Amelia drank in the smell and sight of roses as they walked by a column of them.

"And what did the matter have to do with him?"

"Mr Wrackley is his friend."

Lottie gave her a perceptive look. "You are being unexpectedly forgiving. Does this mean your feelings towards Mr Wrackley have lessened or you have lately warmed to Mr Brightford?"

"Both." Amelia shook her head. "Neither. I do not know."

Lottie sat down on a stone bench set in between two flowerbeds and indicated that Amelia should join her. "Then I think you should tell me absolutely everything that has occurred between you and Mr Brightford since I left."

Lottie's eyes widened when Amelia told her about the slap but she offered no criticism and Amelia explained about the mutual apologies and repeated several amusing comments Mr Brightford had made since then.

"You are falling for him," Lottie pronounced at once, looking pleased at the idea.

Amelia frowned, trying to reconcile all the contradictory feelings she had towards Mr Brightford. "Do you think so?"

"Certainly. A month ago you would have dismissed such comments as ill-mannered and now you find them endearing. You love him."

It was true that she thought well of him now and looked forward to time in his company. "But I have been introduced to him for over a year and known him in passing before that and I never felt anything but irritation towards him. How could I fall in love with him now? The timing is terrible."

"Not necessarily. Seeing my wedding to Alex might give him some ideas."

She smiled at the thought, letting herself imagine for the first time what a future would be like with Mr Brightford, but she only said, "Now you sound like Mrs Gallerton, only she would say it to Mr Brightford's face."

They both shuddered then got to their feet to stroll back to the manor house. Amelia picked a small piece of lavender, rolling it between her fingers and inhaling its scent, considering Mr Brightford's behaviour and hoping his opinion of her had greatly improved in the last week.

Lottie brushed a leaf from her dress and said, "I am glad now that I did not say anything to Mr Wrackley about you."

"Yes, indeed." It would have been awkward if he had decided to court her again but there was certainly no likelihood of that.

* * *

"Why on earth did you write to Wrackley?" Nathan demanded.

Mr Brightford rolled his eyes. He had been relaxing in the library and having a quiet conversation with Alex when Nathan burst in, saying he needed to speak to him alone. The fire was not even lit in the billiards room where they now stood and the evenings were cool. At least Brightford had had the foresight to bring his glass of brandy with him – emotional conversations always made him thirsty. "First you are angry with me for speaking against Miss Daventry to Wrackley and now you are angry when I have tried to put things right."

"But you are in love with her!"

"That is ridiculous." Brightford tried to come up with all the reasons he knew it to be ridiculous as he took a swallow from his brandy. Worryingly, none came to mind. "I like her better than I did but…"

"You love her," Nathan repeated.

"Well, I might feel some… Oh, hell!" Brightford sat down abruptly in a convenient chair as it hit him that his cousin was correct. What a ludicrous turn of events. "In any case, she loves Wrackley and now she can have him."

"She was warming nicely to you before this."

"Nonsense." Brightford took another swig of brandy and choked slightly. Nathan pounded him on the back then patted his shoulder, expression growing sympathetic.

"Well, you will just have to fight him for her."

"You want me to fight a duel?" If this was his idea of a solution then his cousin had been spending far too much time with Harrington.

"No, of course not. I meant that you will have to show her you are the better man for her."

"That would not be fair on Wrackley. They would be engaged by now if not for my interference." Besides, he was not at all sure he was the better man in any way: he was too cynical and bad-tempered. No wonder she preferred someone as charming and handsome as Wrackley. Damn him.

"You do not know that," Fenbridge insisted, "and anyway she did not know you so well then. Could you really bear to see her married to someone else?"

He was not certain he could. He knew that he ought to leave the way clear for Wrackley but could not convince himself to do so. Brightford was a wealthy bachelor; half of Edinburgh's mothers wanted their daughters to catch him. Why then was his romantic life suddenly so infernally complicated?

CHAPTER TWENTY-TWO

"MR WRACKLEY called while you were out riding," Mr Alexander Fenbridge told Amelia when she and Lottie returned from a ride round the estate. "I said he should not wait but he wanted me to convey how sorry he was to have missed you."

Amelia held back a snort with difficulty. She could not imagine why Mr Wrackley would suddenly renew his interest in her - perhaps he was simply bored and in need of a diversion - but she would no longer trust his whims. Besides, she did not want Mr Brightford to think she had feelings for anyone else, not that she was certain of his regard, something that increasingly worried her now she was sure of her own affection. Why could she not have known how she would feel a year ago when she might have avoided all those months of being rude to him?

When Amelia did not immediately respond to his words, Mr Fenbridge smiled at Lottie, full of affection, and asked them both, "How was your ride?"

"Lovely," Amelia said. "You have such a beautiful estate that I will quite envy Lottie living here."

"Then I am sure we both wish that you will be a very frequent visitor," he said, cementing her excellent opinion of him. Mr Fenbridge was not only kind and good-natured but also generous and thoughtful. Amelia might have had doubts at the time but she was beginning to think that Lottie could not have made a wiser choice.

"Nothing could please me more," she said. "And do you have many more guests who will be staying here for your wedding?"

"I have several relatives who are currently in London, who come up to join us in about a week."

As always, the word of that particular city drew her like magic. "Then I hope they are talkative: I would love to hear all that is going on in London at the moment."

"I am sure they will be glad to tell you. Personally, now that Lottie is here with me, I could not be happier anywhere else in the world."

He spoke with quiet sincerity and Lottie gave him a radiant smile. Amelia watched them, a little embarrassed to see such private emotions but more certain than ever that they would be happy together. They suited each other in ways she had never before realised and it occurred to her that this was what real love was like; not the dizzying emotions both she and Lottie had felt in the past.

She hoped with all her heart that they might have both found it for real this time.

* * *

"I expected to hear a report from you when you arrived that you were engaged," Mr Harrington said, frowning, having sent for Benjamin to come to his room for a discussion. Benjamin had known this was coming and the only good thing about it was that he could now get it out of the way. "I presume you do have news on the subject?"

Benjamin met his father's disapproving gaze steadily. "I do indeed. I am not engaged, sir, nor will I ever be. On the contrary, I have formed an attachment with Mr Nathaniel

Fenbridge that precludes any other."

"This is scandalous!" Mr Harrington exclaimed, face flushing with anger.

"Only if society in general finds out about it. I presume you are not planning on making it known?"

"Certainly not. You will break off this disgusting liaison immediately or I will disinherit you and throw you out of my house."

"I love Nathan and he has already said that if you disinherited me I could live here."

"You think Mr Alexander Fenbridge would allow such a thing if he knew the real nature of your relationship with his brother."

"He does know," Benjamin said, strangely calm in the face of his father's fury. "He wishes us happiness together."

His father glowered impotently at him, clearly at a loss now that his greatest threat had not brought Benjamin to heel. "Get out of my sight. I wish I might never see you again."

Benjamin left the room, giving a shaky sigh once he was in the corridor. He went to find Nathan who had been watching a billiards game between his brother and Brightford. Nathan had been there when Benjamin received his summons and left the room to talk to Benjamin in the empty hall.

"I believe I have just been disinherited and disowned," he said.

Nathan put an arm round his shoulder. "Both your parents?"

"Just my father so far. I am sure my mother will soon make her feelings known."

"Perhaps she will be more understanding than you expect."

"I hope so but I doubt it. She has always gone along with whatever he said."

He was acutely aware that he had put his life in

Nathan's hands. There was nothing else left for him.

* * *

"If Mr Wrackley returns do you want to speak to him?" Lottie asked as Amelia admired her wedding dress.

Amelia ran her hand gently over silk covered in finely embroidered lace. "I do not know. Probably not. There seems nothing left to say."

"You thought you loved him before. If he has decided he really does love you in spite of what Mr Brightford said, do you not want to see him so you can test how you feel now?"

"It might be sensible," Amelia conceded with reluctance. She had made a fool of herself before, assuming the mutual interest between her and Mr Wrackley would lead to marriage. Also, her new feelings for Mr Brightford complicated everything and she believed them to be stronger than anything she felt for Mr Wrackley, but unless she saw Mr Wrackley again she could not be certain her feelings for him were gone. Of course, he might not even want to court her - he might just want to apologise for his behaviour before or ask to be friends. "You are so lucky that you are about to marry. It is all far more difficult and less pleasant than I expected it to be. Oh, forgive me," she said as she recalled the early part of the year. "You endured far worse treatment than I from Mr Saverney."

"But that is long over," Lottie said with a serene smile, "and does not cause me any pain. I am where I want to be with the man I want to marry. You are right that I am lucky. More than I have any right to be."

"Now, that is nonsense," Amelia said. "Mr Alexander Fenbridge is luckier than he has any right to be since he will be marrying the kindest, most honourable lady in the world. A life of happiness is exactly what you deserve."

"I could not have been completely happy without my best friend here."

"And I feel far better now I have you to talk to than I have since my father's funeral. I fully intend to hold Mr Alexander Fenbridge to his offer and visit here often until you are both sick of the sight of me."

Lottie laughed. "That is not a thought that worries me."

* * *

"Your father has told me of your peculiar announcement to him regarding yourself and Mr Nathaniel Fenbridge."

Benjamin regarded his mother as she sat embroidering in her room. "I thought he might."

She threw a sharp look at him, the kind that had cowed him as a child. "Do not take that tone with me."

"My apologies, Mother."

"It would be better for you if you gave up this unpleasant behaviour now and returned to our town house."

"I will not."

"If not now, then in time I believe you will change your mind rather than be disinherited and cast out of the family. When that happens I will speak to your father on your behalf."

She said this as if doing him a great favour but it was impossible. He was done with pretence. "I cannot marry. I do not have the necessary feelings towards women."

"I do not know where you and your sister get such romantic ideas about relationships. There are plenty of acceptable marriages where the husband and wife feel nothing more than civility towards each other."

Now that he knew how it felt to be loved the idea of such a heartless marriage repulsed him more than ever.

"You would wish that on me rather than accept my current happiness?"

"It is what society accepts, so it is the only option open to you."

"I am committed to Nathan Fenbridge. I will not give him up."

"We will see."

Benjamin left the interview with his mother feeling more shaken than he had after talking to his father. It hurt that neither of his parents cared enough to accept his relationship with Nathan.

Nathan was waiting for him in Benjamin's bedroom and embraced him. "Did she react any better than your father?"

He gave a bitter laugh. "Hardly." He frowned, abruptly nervous that he had a place in this house. "Are you certain your brother accepts our relationship?"

"Yes, of course." Nathan rubbed his back. "What is wrong?"

"After the way my parents have reacted it seems impossible that other people could possibly allow us to live as we wish."

"Alex has always accepted my feelings about men, Brightford too. Miss Harrington is on your side, is she not?"

Benjamin nodded. "Miss Daventry as well."

"I know it must be difficult not having the support of your parents."

"They never have been," Benjamin realised. They were never able to accept the person he really was. To both of them it would be better if he was living a lie, married and miserable, than happy with a man he loved. "You are all I need, Alex."

He kissed Nathan. The rest of the world could do as it liked as long as he had this man.

* * *

"Mr Wrackley," the butler announced, showing the gentleman into the drawing room.

Mr Brightford instinctively glanced at Miss Daventry, waiting to see what her reaction would be. In this, he had no immediate answer as, after exchanging looks with Miss Harrington, her expression was unreadable.

Alex had got to his feet and greeted Wrackley, who bowed to the ladies and nodded to the men in a friendly fashion, including Brightford. If he blamed Brightford for what had happened in Edinburgh he gave no sign of it.

"It is a pleasure to see you all again," Wrackley said with a smile at Miss Daventry, who glanced down at her tea. Brightford wished he knew what she was thinking. He could not help believing he had acted stupidly, as Nathan had said, in writing to Wrackley, but what else could he honourably have done? Both Wrackley and Miss Daventry deserved happiness. He just wished fervently that they would not find it with each other.

"You do not know all our guests," Alex said to Wrackley. "Allow me to introduce Mrs Gallerton."

This, of course, took some time then the conversation turned to the kind of meaningless small-talk Brightford loathed. He surreptitiously watched Wrackley and Miss Daventry. Wrackley kept glancing at her, trying to catch her eye, while she did not once look at him. Brightford tried not to derive too much hope from that. Certainly Miss Daventry would not give Wrackley an easy time after his desertion but he might still be able to win her over. Particularly if he reminded her that it was all Brightford's fault that he had ever left.

"Would you take a walk with me outside?" Wrackley asked Miss Daventry. He added to her mother, "We will remain within sight of the house, of course."

She hesitated and Brightford could not help hoping she

would refuse. Instead, after receiving a nod from her mother, she smiled at Mr Wrackley and said, "Very well."

CHAPTER TWENTY-THREE

AS SOON AS they left the drawing room, Amelia wished she had not agreed to accompany Mr Wrackley. She felt uncomfortable with him and angry about the way he had vanished without a word to her. However, her conversation with Lottie on the matter had convinced her she ought to hear what he wanted to say and then see how she felt about him. If she was supposed to do this then she was making a poor start as all she could think about was the uneasy expression she had seen on Mr Brightford's face when they had left.

They walked out into the garden and Mr Wrackley at once turned to her. "Miss Daventry, I owe you the deepest of apologies and an explanation of my behaviour in Edinburgh."

Not wanting to hear Mr Brightford's disparaging words about her again, she hastily said, "I have been made aware that you heard ill of my character."

"I should never have listened," he said. "When we met I felt the greatest admiration for your character and beauty. I should have trusted my feelings instead of listening to… to anyone else."

"In Edinburgh I liked your company a great deal but a

lot has happened since then…"

"I heard about your father," he interrupted, frowning. "I cannot bear to think that my behaviour made your grief after his death even more painful. I am so sorry."

She could tell he was speaking sincerely and was glad, after all, that she had heard him. However, her previous feelings for him still failed to reappear. "I accept your apology but, as I was saying, a lot has changed. I do not feel that I am the same person I was then and I do not wish to mislead you."

"Then can we begin again as if we had just met?"

"Certainly," she agreed with relief.

They returned to the drawing room where the curiosity on everyone's faces that they were unable to express was almost comical. Amelia avoided looking at Mr Brightford, feeling guilty which was ridiculous. She had just talked to Mr Wrackley. Nothing more. Besides, she had no idea if Mr Brightford genuinely did have any interest in her; his expressions were so difficult to read.

The conversation continued for another half hour or so then the gentlemen headed outside to do some shooting.

Amelia and Lottie managed to escape from Mrs Gallerton and, the moment they were alone in Amelia's room, Lottie asked, "What happened with Mr Wrackley?"

"He apologised and I accepted. We were both very polite…"

"Then your feelings for him are gone?"

Amelia was not sure how her saying they had been polite had conveyed her lack of interest in Mr Wrackley but since that was the truth she did not question it. Lottie knew her better than anyone. "I believe so. I still look at him and find him attractive but it does not touch my heart as it did before."

"I think you should give yourself a bit of time," Lottie said, sitting on the bed. "You are still grieving for your father and that is bound to affect your emotions."

"I certainly feel muddle-headed."

"Then put it from your mind for the moment. You have several weeks here to get to know both Mr Wrackley and Mr Brightford and see how you feel."

"And how he- they feel."

* * *

Mr Brightford cared nothing for her.

That was the opinion she had formed several days later. He had made no effort to seek out her company. If he did run into her he was polite but nothing more than that. Once again it seemed that she had made a fool of herself.

This humiliation was reduced by Mr Wrackley's frequent presence. At least he thought highly of her, even if he had not consistently done so. But she could understand why he had put faith in the words of Mr Brightford, whom he had known for a great deal longer than he had known her, so she was willing to trust him again. Any fond feelings, however, failed to re-emerge.

"It is as if something inside me wants me to be miserable," she told Lottie angrily as they walked along a path in the wood behind the house. "I want Mr Wrackley who then vanishes. Then I want Mr Brightford, who has never had the tiniest interest in me. Then Mr Wrackley is in my life again but I do not want him after all."

"You cannot make decisions that will last the rest of your life after a few days," Lottie insisted. "Forget about both of them for a while."

"I cannot when they are both constantly right in front of me!"

* * *

Brightford had never been so vexed in his life.

He was trying to give Miss Daventry time alone with Wrackley but all his instincts were yelling at him to fight to win her for himself.

He had no idea how the courtship was progressing and could hardly ask either of its participants. Not that he wanted to know. Unless it was not progressing, which he would love to know.

"You look in a devil of a mood," a voice told him and he glanced round to see Harrington approaching, for once alone.

"It is your Nathan's fault for putting the idea in my head that I should court Miss Daventry."

"Well, it would seem stupid not to when you are in love with her," Harrington said easily, coming to lean his arms on the fence in front of them and watch the horses within.

"Then I suppose I am a fool," he ground out. "It is a matter of honour."

"Then she will probably spurn both of you and find someone else entirely."

Brightford glared at him. "Do you not have somewhere else you need to be?"

Harrington shook his head, expression innocent save for an amused glint in his eyes.

CHAPTER TWENTY-FOUR

"I BELIEVE YOU have behaved like a cad, sir," Wrackley told Brightford stiffly.

They were outside the house but there were enough grooms and other workers about that Brightford headed further away so they would not be overheard talking. Clearly he had been wrong when he believed that Wrackley held no ill-will towards him anymore, but being called a cad seemed an extreme reaction.

"I have apologised to both you and Miss Daventry for what I said to you…"

"I do not doubt that," Wrackley interrupted, clearly wound up. "You could not have made your interest more plain."

"My what?" They had neared a field containing several horses and one trotted up to the fence to look them over.

"Do not pretend with me, Brightford. You put me off Miss Daventry so you could court her yourself."

"No, I did not," he answered, stung that someone he had always considered a friend could believe him capable of such a thing. "I believed what I said at the time and only found out later that I had been wrong."

"You cannot tell me that you do not have feelings for

her?"

"No, I cannot, but I have done my best to keep my distance from her because you might have been engaged to her by now had I not interfered."

"I see." Wrackley looked uncomfortable. He bent down a picked a handful of grass which he held out to the sorrel mare. After a moment she approached and took it from him. "I apologise. I spoke like a fool."

"Yes, well, you are in love. I believe acting like a fool is a requirement of the condition."

Wrackley laughed and stroked the sorrel's nose. "This is an awkward situation."

"Not at all. I believe the lady is in love with you and you with her. It seems very simple."

"I am not so sure of her feelings. Besides, I want Miss Daventry to want me alone. She cannot choose me if there is no choice."

"I am not following you."

"You should court her too and let her decide for herself who she wants. That way we will both know that the man she finally chooses is who she really wants."

Brightford nodded. A fair fight was all he wanted. "Agreed."

* * *

"Mr Wrackley will be an excellent husband for you," Mrs Gallerton said in a satisfied tone as if she was somehow responsible for this interest.

Amelia exchanged a glance with her mother and said, "Mr Wrackley has not asked me to marry him and even if he did I am not certain I would accept.

"I thought you liked him," her mother said, clearly having thought that Amelia was happy to be courted by Mr Wrackley.

Mrs Gallerton simultaneously made an annoyed sound

which Amelia ignored, saying, "I do like him but I am not sure that that is enough."

"It is an excellent match," Mrs Gallerton insisted, adopting the firm tone that never failed to annoy Amelia, "and I know the state of your family's finances. When he asks you must accept him."

Amelia took a deep breath and said as calmly as she was able, "I believe that is my decision, Aunt."

"If you turn him down then you will be responsible for your family's ruin and do not expect me to support you both."

"We expect nothing of the kind," Mrs Daventry said to her. "If Amelia does not marry Mr Wrackley then we will manage. He is not the only man in the world and she is still a young girl."

"Hmm." Mrs Gallerton looked angrily from one to the other of them, her glare settling on Amelia. "If you are holding out for Mr Brightford then you are wasting your time. He clearly has no intention of being caught."

Amelia put down her book and excused herself. She left the house and kept walking as fast as she could until she was out of breath and the house was the size of a toy behind her. Even worse than her hopes being so transparent was the suspicion that Mrs Gallerton was correct.

CHAPTER TWENTY-FIVE

AMELIA HAD slept badly the previous night and by the end of it was convinced that Mr Brightford had no interest in her at all. Therefore, to come down to breakfast and find him determined to sit at her side and converse solely with her was more confusing than pleasant, particularly when Mrs Gallerton kept glaring at her as if she were flirting outrageously with him rather than politely answering his inquiries.

"It is a shame that you will not be able to dance at the ball tonight," he said, referring of course to the fact Amelia and her mother were in mourning. It was Mr Wrackley who was hosting the ball on his estate.

"Yes," she agreed, aware that Mrs Gallerton was listening to every word with narrowed eyes. "However, I find that balls also give a good opportunity to converse with new people."

"Only with new people?" he asked with mock concern.

"Indeed," she said, equally lightly. "I will certainly not wish to talk to anyone I know."

He laughed and Mrs Gallerton's glower deepened. "Then I must make the most of the chance to speak with you while I am allowed."

"Perhaps you might extend the conversation," Mr Nathaniel Fenbridge suggested with a smile. "Harrington and I were just saying that today looks set to be a brief return to balmy weather before the autumn arrives. We thought that anyone who wishes might care to join us for a short walk followed by a picnic."

The rest of the group, including Amelia, agreed to this.

* * *

"You do believe that Mr Brightford has serious intentions towards Amelia, do you not?" Lottie asked her fiancé as they left the house to join the others. "His interest does not always seem constant."

"I believe he loves her but he has not spoken of it to me. I thought she preferred Mr Wrackley?"

"If he had not vanished from Edinburgh without a word then I am sure she would have accepted a proposal from him. When he left her father died and her life grew a lot more complicated. Mr Brightford was there when others, including myself, were not."

"So she loves Jolly?"

"I think that if she knew how he felt she would be able to make up her mind."

"The same argument could be used for him," he offered. "Perhaps we should leave it to them to resolve."

Lottie could not be satisfied with this. She remembered how much she had suffered from Mr Saverney's treatment and now Amelia was in a slightly similar position. Neither Mr Wrackley nor Mr Brightford were consistently affectionate for long enough for Amelia to be sure either one would propose. Lottie was worried for her friend, particularly when she was still grieving for her father. The men were not being fair to her and Lottie did not want to see her hurt.

* * *

"What a lovely estate you have," Mrs Gallerton said to Mr Wrackley. "Any woman would be lucky indeed to be mistress of such a home." She threw a meaningful look at Miss Daventry who gave a polite smile but flushed uncomfortably at the pointed comment.

Mr Brightford had been worried that the ball here might charm Miss Daventry into looking more favourably upon Wrackley, but as the evening's entertainments began he started to hope it might have the opposite effect. Wrackley, after all, could not dance with Miss Daventry because she was in mourning but he was duty bound to dance with other ladies, which kept him away from her for much of the time.

He could also see that Mrs Gallerton's many unsubtle comments were having the opposite of their desired effect and irritating Miss Daventry. The more Mrs Gallerton spoke the less Miss Daventry seemed to want to be here or spend time with Wrackley. Thank goodness Brightford had fallen for a woman with such a delightfully contrary nature.

Brightford had spent enough time staying with his cousins that he knew around half of the three dozen people at the ball, the group easily fitting into the grand ballroom, so he was caught up in answering enquiries about his health and about Edinburgh for some time. He avoided dancing, though, as there was only one lady he wanted to stand up with and that was impossible this evening. Also, he would not want her to see him dancing with someone else and think his attentions fickle; there had been enough disagreements and misunderstandings between them.

After a couple of hours Brightford saw Mrs Gallerton distracted by an introduction to another of the neighbourhood's families, so he headed quickly to Miss Daventry's side. "It is growing rather stuffy with so many people here," he commented. "Would you and Miss Harrington care to take a stroll outside. I believe the gardens are quite picturesque in the moonlight."

Miss Daventry glanced at Miss Harrington who gave a slight shrug that left the decision up to her. Miss Daventry gave him a bright smile that knocked the breath clean out of his body. "That would be lovely."

They headed out, Alex joining them, and Brightford caught a glare from Wrackley. Well, the man had said it was up to Miss Daventry to choose between them. It was a fair fight now and one Brightford was determined to win for the sake of his own future happiness.

"Oh, how beautiful," Miss Harrington exclaimed as she saw the gardens brightened by a full moon and lit with dozens of lanterns.

"It is like magic," Miss Daventry said.

Brightford had never seen the expression of wonder on her face before and smiled, touched. Miss Harrington took Alex's arm and Miss Daventry took his as they strolled round. A few other couples or groups were doing the same but otherwise, after the noise and movement in the hall, the evening was still and peaceful. They even heard the hoot of a nearby owl.

Brightford let the setting inspire him, sharing light banter with Miss Daventry and offering her several compliments. When they returned to Alex's home in the early hours of the morning he believed he had made a positive impression – hopefully helping to dismiss from her mind their earlier quarrels – and he was satisfied that Miss Daventry could not fail to understand his intentions.

CHAPTER TWENTY-SIX

"YOUR BEHAVIOUR last night was abominable!" Mrs Gallerton scolded Amelia.

They were alone in the drawing room as the men were, as usual, out shooting while Lottie had had to leave to see to some household matters and Mrs Harrington and Mama had letters to compose. At least that was what Mama had said but Amelia suspected that she had just wanted to escape Mrs Gallerton's company for an hour or two. Amelia had known Mrs Gallerton for less than two months and did not appreciate being taken to task by her.

"I can think of nothing I did that would warrant your saying that," she responded, keeping her eyes fixed on her embroidery.

"You led Mr Wrackley on a merry chase vanishing off with Mr Brightford like that."

Amelia gritted her teeth. "I went for a walk outside with three other people, one of whom was Mr Brightford. There was nothing in the least unladylike in that."

"Mr Wrackley was not pleased…"

"Mr Wrackley's feelings do not concern me," she snapped.

"Nor do mine, I suppose."

Amelia did not answer and the two of them glared at each other.

"The trouble with you is that you want to be the centre of attention and you use your beauty to achieve it," Mrs Gallerton said. "You would rather flirt with first one man then another and think you will get away with such games…"

"…I do not!"

"… But you cannot and such behaviour will lose you both men…"

"Madam, you are not my mother and I will not be lectured by you. I am not playing games with anyone - I simply wish to choose a future that will bring me happiness not blindly agree to marry the first man who looks at me."

"You will end up an old maid."

She returned her aunt's glower. "If that happens then I will make the best of it. I want to live my life, not hide away, letting a man make every decision for me and letting the gossip of women cower me."

"Do not be so naïve. You live in a world where men are the masters of their households and where the judgement of society can ruin a woman's life. You cannot give in to Mr Brightford's sudden flattery. I believe he is just toying with you."

Amelia hated the possibility that this might be true. She did not know what to do for the best. "I appreciate your advice, Aunt, but I must decide what to do for myself."

"This stubbornness is unladylike."

"Perhaps so," Amelia agreed, abruptly seeing the humour in such a comment from Mrs Gallerton, "but I believe it runs in our family."

She was spared any further conversation by Lottie's return and the two of them went for a stroll around the gardens. Amelia told Lottie what her aunt had said and begged her advice.

"I feel sure Mr Wrackley will ask me to marry him

soon," Amelia said, "although I have been wrong about that before."

"I am certain he will too," Lottie said, "but I thought your feelings for him were tepid."

"They are but I like him well enough. I do not think I would be unhappy with him and you would be close by which would be a great advantage."

Lottie stopped beside a statue. "Why would you think of marrying him when you love Mr Brightford?"

Amelia sighed gustily. "I have not seen Mr Brightford all morning and cannot be certain of his regard. He barely spoke to me when we first got here. Indeed his attentiveness comes and goes in the most unreliable manner. If I only had myself to think about I would not think of marrying without love but I must consider my family's position. If I do not make a good match quickly then we could face financial ruin. We have already been urged by our man of business to sell our estate but Mama would not hear of it and I cannot bear to see her further distressed."

"My poor friend." Lottie put an arm round Amelia's shoulders. "I had no idea you had had so much to worry about lately on top of your grief over your father."

Amelia felt tears pricking her eyes at this sympathy and blinked them back. Her father's death still hurt more than she could put into words but she needed to put such thoughts to one side and make a decision. "I have no idea what I should do, Lottie."

* * *

Mr Brightford returned to the house with the other men for a late luncheon to discover that Mr Wrackley had called upon Miss Daventry and they were out walking together, with Miss Harrington acting as chaperone. Why could Mrs Gallerton not have gone along as chaperone and prevented them from getting any pleasure from the excursion?

The thought of what Wrackley was saying to win Miss Daventry's affection plagued him. His heart told him to ask her to marry him before Wrackley could do so, but his sense of honour would not allow it. It was not fair to demand Miss Daventry make such an important decision when her mind was still soaked with grief over the loss of her father. He saw every day how much she and her mother suffered and they should be allowed as much time as they needed to recover.

Brightford's intentions must be clear to Miss Daventry by now, so he would wait until they returned to Edinburgh. Then the decision of who to accept was hers. He was confident about her answer.

Fairly confident.

He had no idea whatsoever what her answer would be and that, along with Wrackley's presence, was driving him half insane.

He went in search of the other men and suggested a ride, hoping that the exercise would distract him. Nathan, of course, insisted that his fiancée might wish to join them and, when asked, Wrackley and Miss Daventry thought it sounded a pleasant idea too. So much for a distraction...

CHAPTER TWENTY-SEVEN

THE SUN WAS shining and the world had never looked more beautiful to Lottie as she sat beside her father in the carriage on the way to be married.

"You are not too nervous?" her father checked.

Lottie knew that brides were supposed to be scared before they got married but all she felt this morning was happiness. Mr Alexander Fenbridge was the best man she had ever met and she wanted to be married to him and begin their shared life. A month ago she might not have been sure of him but the more time they spent together the luckier she felt. She smiled at her father. "I am not nervous in the least."

He patted her hand. "Good girl. Your mother and I are proud that you have done so well for yourself. Fenbridge is an excellent man in every way."

"He is," she agreed, not certain that she deserved any credit for the marriage. She had not set out to secure Alex's attentions; she had just enjoyed his company and matters had progressed from there. Her present joy was entirely due to him.

"You coped well with your past disappointment," her father continued and she gave an involuntary shiver, the reminder of her previous engagement like an ill omen.

"There is the church," she said quickly as the building came into view.

"It is not very large."

She had not told her parents that Alex had offered to give her a grand wedding in a cathedral but that she had preferred his local church and the jovial vicar in charge of it. She knew her parents would have wanted all the grandeur possible but this was her wedding and, for once, she had focused solely on what would please Alex and herself. She could not regret it.

Her father helped her down from the carriage and she felt a moment's panic - what if Alex had changed his mind and was not inside? A few village children waited outside to catch a glimpse of her wedding dress before ducking back into the church for the service and their smiling faces reassured her. The past was over and she trusted Alex.

Music began to play and her father led her inside. Lottie saw Alex at once and when he turned round his face lit up at the sight of her. She felt none of her old fears at being the centre of attention; Alex gave her courage as he always had. All she saw was him for the rest of the ceremony and then she was Mrs Fenbridge and everyone was congratulating them both.

Lottie felt almost overwhelmed by happiness.

* * *

Amelia turned round on the church bench when Lottie and her father entered the church. Lottie looked beautiful in her wedding outfit and the wedding was like something from a fairytale with the couple gazing lovingly at each other as they said their vows. Afterwards Amelia joined in cheering for them and throwing rice as they rode off in their carriage together.

She was still smiling as her party followed the wedded

couple back to the Fenbridge estate. Her mother had agreed that they should wear normal dresses, instead of their mourning outfits, just for the day and it was nice to feel pretty again and to not have to worry that her outfit would bring down everyone else's mood. As they drove along Mr Brightford caught her eye and smiled at her and she could not remember a more enjoyable day.

When they were in the hall of Mr Alexander Fenbridge's house and Amelia had hugged the bride and told her how perfect she looked, Mr Brightford approached her through the throng of chattering people. He bowed to her and she curtsied.

"I would ask you to dance but I know your mother would not allow that during the mourning period," he said.

"No. It is impossible at the moment but I feel almost a different person not wearing black today."

"You look enchanting."

"Thank you good sir," she said with mock-demureness.

"I am *good* today: that is progress."

She laughed. "I do not recall ever saying you were not good. It must be your own guilty conscience putting the idea into your head."

"Touche!"

They were prevented from conversing further by the arrival of Mr Wrackley, his many siblings with him. There followed various polite conversations then Mr Wrackley asked if he could speak to her. When they were alone outside he went down on one knee and Amelia's heart sank. The day had been so promising until now.

She knew that the sensible response would be to accept him but, despite her earlier feelings, she no longer wished to marry anyone but Mr Brightford. Who had not asked her.

Mr Wrackley's proposal was eloquent and seemed heartfelt so it upset her to think of hurting him as she did genuinely like him, but she could not deceive him. "I am flattered more than I can express at your proposal…" she began.

Perhaps he heard the refusal in her tone as he quickly said, "You need not give me an immediate answer. Would you think it over? I know my behaviour in Edinburgh is against me…"

Now it was her turn to interrupt him. "Not at all. I am only grateful your friends convinced you that my character was not so terrible as you have been led to think."

"Mr Brightford."

She was confused. Why would he mention his rival at such a moment? "Excuse me?"

"It was Mr Brightford who wrote to me that he had been utterly wrong about you."

Amelia stared at him, the day darkening as she took in his words. If Mr Brightford had encouraged Mr Wrackley to renew his courtship then he could have no serious feelings for her himself. His friendliness towards her these recent weeks had apparently meant nothing.

CHAPTER TWENTY-EIGHT

MR BRIGHTFORD had been less than delighted to discover that Mr Wrackley intended to travel with the parties back to Edinburgh to stay with the Harrington family. Mrs Fenbridge's parents would return in one carriage while the rest of the group would share another, which would hardly give him a chance to speak to Miss Daventry privately.

He brightened at the thought that if it was clear how he and Miss Daventry felt about each other then perhaps Wrackley would admit defeat and leave again. This pleasant dream, alas, did not last even until Alex's estate was out of sight, Wrackley's behaviour towards her just as attentive and warm as ever. Miss Daventry, however, looked weighed down by burdens today, the happy, witty lady at yesterday's wedding entirely gone. Perhaps the return to Edinburgh was a painful reminder of her father's loss or maybe she was recalling her family's financial difficulties. He did not know the extent of the problem but was sure he could find some way to help them.

"I believe Mr Harrington offered some assistance to you in the matter of the late Mr Daventry's affairs," Brightford ventured, gaining a suspicious look from

Wrackley. "I would be happy to humbly offer my own advice over such matters."

"That is kind of you…" Mrs Daventry began then glanced at her daughter.

Miss Daventry took over the sentence, saying to him with a cool glance, "However, we will not be staying in Edinburgh. We will go to our country estate almost at once."

Brightford's only consolation from this blow was that Wrackley looked just as horrified as he felt. Even Mrs Gallerton looked as if she knew nothing of this plan, which was strange.

"You will not be gone long, I hope," Wrackley said.

"Perhaps a month," Mrs Daventry said.

"Or a little longer," Miss Daventry said. "There may be a number of matters that need to be resolved while we are there."

Well, that could not be any more vague. Financial matters? Farming matters? Yet another suitor?

"I had not expected to be subjected to more exhausting travelling," Mrs Gallerton complained.

"We would be sorry indeed if it cut short your visit to us," Mrs Daventry said, sounding admirably sincere. "However, we would understand if you wished to return home before the winter sets in."

"I suppose it would be pleasant to see the estate where I grew up again," Mrs Gallerton mused and Miss Daventry's face fell in a manner that would have been amusing in other circumstances. "I recall it is not too great a distance from Edinburgh."

Brightford watched Miss Daventry as her mother reassured Mrs Gallerton, who apparently had no intention of going home any time soon. All had been friendly between him and Miss Daventry at the wedding but she had avoided his eye ever since getting into the carriage. Could she have decided to accept Mr Wrackley? No, he realised with relief, there would have been no need to vanish to the country if that were the case. Then what had changed between them in less than a day?

She was looking out of the window now, her reflection resembling that of a ghost, pale and sad.

CHAPTER TWENTY-NINE

IT HAD BEEN nearly two months since he had last laid eyes on Miss Daventry. She had apparently not been at home when he called on her in Edinburgh - something he was not certain he believed. After that she, her mother and Mrs Gallerton had vanished to their country estate and there had been no word or sign of them since.

It was enough to drive a man mad. He paced up and down his library until a tentative knock upon the door distracted him.

"Yes?"

His Tiger stepped through the door, with an expression that said he expected to be killed on the spot for coming inside the house.

"You have news?" Brightford asked, all his focus upon the fidgeting boy.

"She's back, sir. Miss Daventry. The whole family, I mean. Their carriage is there and one of the maids confirmed it."

At last! Brightford thanked the boy and strode upstairs to change into a more suitable outfit for calling upon a young lady. Twenty minutes later he was being announced at Mrs Daventry's home.

He stepped into the drawing room to the unpleasant sight of a room full of people.

"Brightford."

"Alex?" He shook his cousin's hand, the expression on Alex's face that of a man entirely happy with his life. Well, that was excellent, but could not Alex have given him a chance to be similarly content before reappearing?

He belatedly bowed to the ladies present, tearing his gaze from Miss Daventry to respectfully acknowledge the others. Good lord, was that vivacious, stylish woman Miss Harrington? Or rather, Mrs Fenbridge. No wonder Alex was beaming all over the place.

There could be no hope of speaking privately to Miss Daventry now so he reluctantly exerted himself to be charming. He feigned interest in the sights seen in London during the honeymoon while Miss Daventry spoke only to Mrs Fenbridge.

Just as it felt as if the situation could get no worse the butler stepped into the room: "Mr Wrackley," he announced.

* * *

Amelia closed the bedroom door behind her so she and Lottie could have some privacy.

"Oh, you look so lovely," she said, taking in Lottie's extravagant travelling outfit and feathered hat. "Have you bought a lot of clothes?"

Lottie laughed. "I have. I would have been content with a couple of outfits but Mr Fenbridge insisted that I have an entirely new wardrobe provided by the best modiste in London."

Amelia sighed in delight.

"Oh, it is not that that matters. He has been so kind and wonderful. I am happier than I have ever been in my life."

"You love him," Amelia realised. How had Lottie fallen in love *after* getting married? Would that happen to her if she accepted Mr Wrackley? Was she worrying about what to do unnecessarily?

"I do," Lottie was saying, leaning back in the chair, sophisticated and radiant. "I did not understand what love really was until I met Alex. And what of you? How many gentlemen have asked you to marry them?"

"Just Mr Wrackley," she confessed.

"So you have turned him down?"

"Not yet. He is a good man but I do not love him. Do you think that could be enough?"

Lottie frowned. "What of Mr Brightford? I thought your true feelings were for him?"

"That is immaterial. I do not believe he ever intended to propose to me."

"Then how dare he pay court to you the entire time he was at our estate. What was he thinking?"

Amelia swallowed, the subject still almost too painful to contemplate. "I suppose he was bored and wanted a brief dalliance."

"It is unbelievable." Lottie shook her head. "Are you absolutely certain of this?"

"I know that he wrote to Mr Wrackley to convince him to resume his courtship. Could he possibly have done that if he wanted to marry me himself?"

"I think you will have to tell me exactly what both men have said to you," Lottie responded.

If anyone could help her resolve this it was Lottie. So Amelia made herself comfortable on her chair and did exactly that, explaining all that had been said and her own feelings and conclusions on the matter. Then she turned to her friend for a solution.

"You must confront Mr Brightford," said the woman who resembled Amelia's old friend Lottie but sounded far more confident. "Either he did wish to marry you and botched everything in the worst way imaginable or he did not, in which case I think it would be entirely reasonable for you to slap him again. Hard."

CHAPTER THIRTY

"I HAVE NEVER seen you looking so well," Brightford told his cousin as they began a game of billiards. Alex and Mrs Fenbridge were staying with her parents for a few weeks after their honeymoon, catching up with friends and family; some of their family, anyway, as apparently Nathan and Harrington were thoroughly settled at Alex's estate and keeping everything running efficiently there.

"Marrying Lottie is the best thing I did in my life," Alex said. "She is perfect."

Brightford wondered what it said about his character that perfection sounded a little dull to him. But then all ladies seemed dull in comparison to Miss Daventry. Even her mourning clothes could not diminish her beauty and she seemed more composed than she had at Alex's estate, perhaps now beginning to put her grief behind her. He recalled the frivolous girl she had been last year and thought she had matured into a strong-willed, kind, intelligent woman. Now would be the perfect time to ask her to marry him – if only she did not hate him so much.

Alex took his shot and the balls scattered across the table. "I gather you do not wish to marry Miss Daventry after all," he observed with a note of criticism in his tone.

"What makes you suppose that?" Brightford demanded. "I could not get near her. She has been away in the country this entire time."

"That does not seem to have stopped Wrackley."

Brightford lowered his billiards cue. "What do you mean?"

"Apparently he proposed to Miss Daventry some while ago and has an interview with her tomorrow morning to hear her reply."

Brightford put down his cue and headed for the door. "Forgive me for deserting you, Alex, but I can't lose her now."

He ordered his carriage to be brought to the front of the house, keen to leave. He could be happy with no one but Miss Daventry and he had to resolve whatever had gone wrong between them.

* * *

Amelia had been enjoying a good morning until Mr Brightford arrived. Having spent her stay in the country wondering if they would have to sell the estate, she and her mother had returned here to be told by their man of business that her father had made an investment he had not known about, which meant they were far better off than they had thought. They were still far from wealthy but they could manage on the money now.

She and her mother had only just returned from this meeting when Mr Brightford had appeared, clearly in a bad mood, and asked with the barest of civility if she would accompany him on a drive around the park. She had been tempted to say no but was too curious as to his reason. Besides, she had thought of him a good deal while she was away and it was pleasant to once again see his face even if he was scowling... Why was he scowling at her when he was the one who was in the wrong?

"I understand that Mr Wrackley is to see you tomorrow to get an answer to his proposal. I was not even aware he had asked."

The hateful man spoke accusingly as if she were the one who had behaved cruelly, not he. Indeed, it was almost enough to convince her to accept Mr Wrackley. At least that gentleman could behave in a courteous manner. He had accepted without complaint that she did not feel able to answer his proposal until she returned to Edinburgh from the country and his devotion was all that a woman could wish for. If only her emotions were not just as muddled as they had been two months ago. And the cause of that confusion dared to sit there demanding answers.

"I am not aware that the matter could possibly be considered your business," she informed him in her most quelling tone.

He glared at her. "You astonish me, madam."

She returned his glare, more furious by the second. "Since you have not made me any offer yourself and I am given to understand that you have no intention of doing so…"

"What are you saying?" His shock changed her emotions in an instant, hope coursing through her. "If I had had the opportunity to do so, of course I would have made you an offer. How could you possibly doubt it?"

Amelia's knees went weak and it was fortunate that she was sitting down in the carriage. Unaccountably, she had an inconvenient desire to burst into tears. She took a deep breath and spoke as calmly as she was able. "I was informed that you had encouraged Mr Wrackley's courtship of me."

"Well, yes, I did."

She gasped. "Then your behaviour, sir, is utterly incomprehensible!"

"Not in the least," he responded in a stiff manner. "It was my fault that he did not make you an offer when he first visited Edinburgh. Since my opinion about you then was wrong, my honour demanded that I inform him of the fact."

"Your honour? What of your duty not to make me utterly miserable? And how calmly you speak of having thought me cold-hearted and mercenary as if it were the tiniest of mistakes."

"The failure was not all mine," he objected. "If your behaviour had been more demure…"

From between gritted teeth she managed to demand, "Take me home now!"

He did so, neither of them saying a word to each other during the journey. Finally, as he handed her down from the carriage, he said, "My words did not come out as I intended…"

"Indeed?" she queried sweetly. "Perhaps you should take lessons from Mr Wrackley: I have always found him to be most eloquent. Should you see him today pray do inform him of how much I look forward to our conversation tomorrow. Good day, sir."

She marched up to her door which their butler opened instantly. Ignoring Mrs Gallerton's voice coming from the drawing room Amelia ran up to her room and shut her door behind her, flinging herself down on her bed.

How dare he criticise her for not being *demure*?

She sat up and put a hand over her mouth as the more important fact sank in.

He had always meant to ask her to marry him.

CHAPTER THIRTY-ONE

"I AM SO glad that you are back to help me sort out the disastrous mess of my life."

Lottie smiled at the melodramatic statement, although she did not blame Amelia in the least for feeling like this given what she had just revealed about Mr Brightford. They were sitting in the sewing room with the rain beating against the window and the fragrance of cooking bread wafting in from the kitchen. It was almost like old times, except that Lottie was not the timid creature she used to be. In the whole time they had known each other Alex had never once criticised her; on the contrary, they were in agreement on every subject and he complimented her on everything she did. His love gave her the confidence to speak her mind and to take pleasure in every part of her life.

"At least now you know that he was genuinely courting you," she said.

Amelia grimaced. "And was apparently so confident of himself that he threw a rival at me for his own amusement."

"I am sure that was not the case," Lottie said, "although Mr Brightford's idea of behaving honourably is rather vexing."

"And his feelings clearly change from one moment to the next," Amelia exclaimed, still clearly furious from her conversation with the gentleman in question earlier today. "A few months ago he apparently hated me."

"A few months ago you also loathed him."

"That is not... Very well, that is pertinent, but must he be so tactless? Has he no idea at all of how to conduct a courtship?"

"Apparently not."

"Well, I am still tempted to marry Mr Wrackley just to pay Mr Brightford back for his unchivalrous behaviour."

"I believe that if you did so you would be injuring yourself as much as him."

"Oh, I do not mean it," Amelia relented, "but I regret that I have given Mr Wrackley hope all this time when I must now find a way to turn him down. I believe he also loves me."

"I am certain of it, although he too has not always acted as he should."

"Which is also Mr Brightford's fault."

Lottie saw the annoyance simmering again in Amelia's expression and was heartily glad that her own relationship with Mr Fenbridge was free from such a tempestuous side. She was beginning to wonder if Amelia and Mr Brightford's relationship would ever reach a happy conclusion. Perhaps it would have been better for them both to have never formed a tendre.

"How is your mother?"

Amelia brightened and smiled. "She has been much more her old self ever since we visited you for your wedding. She still misses Papa, of course, but I believe we are both moving forward with our lives now. Have you seen anything of your brother?"

"We returned home for a week before coming to see you. I believe Benjy is nearly as happy with Mr Nathaniel Fenbridge as I am with Alex. They are very much in love."

"That is wonderful."

"It is and good luck, like bad, is supposed to run in threes," Lottie insisted, determined her friend should find happiness. "It is now your turn."

CHAPTER THIRTY-TWO

MR WRACKLEY is paying a call on you this morning, is he not?" Mrs Daventry said over breakfast, although she could hardly have been in any doubt over the matter.

Mrs Gallerton was, thankfully, not awake at this hour to join them and to put forward her own many opinions on the subject. Amelia could imagine just what she would say in any case. Amelia was worried about speaking to Mr Wrackley and hurting his feelings and also concerned that her mother would not understand why she was doing this.

She composed herself for a moment then said, "I intend to turn him down, Mama."

"I thought as much." Mrs Daventry gave a calm nod and went back to her breakfast.

Amelia closed her mouth on the long explanation she had intended to give in defence of her actions and hoped that Mr Wrackley would take the news so well.

* * *

Mr Brightford took the fob watch from his pocket and

examined the time for around the thirtieth occasion this morning. By now Mr Wrackley would probably be speaking to Miss Daventry and he had no idea what her answer would be to him. Why had he sent Wrackley that blasted letter encouraging him to resume his courtship? How could he have behaved with such stupidity?

And if only he had known that Miss Daventry thought he did not mean to propose he could have denied this error and got in his own proposal by now.

And why was it that he could never have a conversation with her that did not result in the two of them losing their tempers with each other? It had become the most annoying and counter-productive of habits. If it had not somehow happened yesterday he could still have made her an offer.

At least she now knew he intended to do so. Surely that would make a difference to her decision?

He took his watch once more from his pocket and stared at it.

* * *

"It greatly distresses me to have to cause you pain but I cannot marry you," Amelia told Mr Wrackley as they stood in the drawing room. "I like you a great deal but my feelings are no stronger than that."

"They might grow with time," he said, still holding her hand.

Having seen Lottie's happiness with Mr Alexander Fenbridge, she believed that what he was saying was possible. It might well have convinced her to marry him were her heart not already lost to the most exasperating man in the world.

She squeezed his hand, letting her regret show, then drew away. "I am so sorry, but my answer is no."

* * *

Mr Brightford grabbed a book from the shelves of his library when he heard the knock upon his front door. He threw himself down into a chair and looked down at the book, then hastily turned it the right way round, just as his cousin entered the room.

"Mrs Fenbridge and I happened to run into Wrackley on our way back from the park," Alex said, taking a seat opposite.

Brightford's hands clenched around the book. "Oh?"

Alex's mouth twitched. "We offered him our commiserations."

"Indeed." Brightford let out a shaky breath and resisted the urge to give a cheer at this news.

"I will leave you to your reading." Alex got up and headed for the door, glancing back from the doorway. "A lady like that will not be without suitors for long. For goodness' sakes, stop dithering and offer for her."

CHAPTER THIRTY-THREE

"IS SHE GOING to be there tonight?" Brightford asked when Alex walked into the library. A dinner party had never before interested him so much.

Alex shrugged. "My wife will not tell me. It seems she believes you have ill-treated her friend and deserve no assistance in putting matters right."

"But I must go out of town for a day or two tomorrow on an urgent matter for my estate. If I do not see Miss Daventry tonight I might not see her for several days and by then she might be too vexed to speak to me."

"That makes things difficult," Alex agreed with an utter lack of concern.

"Could you not convince your wife..?"

"No." Alex got to his feet and patted Brightford's shoulder. "I am sure you will be able to sort matters out on your own. Despite past proof to the contrary."

Brightford gave his cousin a thin smile – so much for getting any assistance from him.

* * *

"I wish I could wear some colour of dress other than black to the dinner party tonight," Amelia told Lottie as she admired the evening gown her friend intended to wear. "I am, of course, still grieving Papa - indeed I think I always shall - but I do not see why I have to look ugly while doing so."

"You could not possibly look ugly and I doubt Mr Brightford will care what you are wearing."

"You have still not told him I will be there?"

"Of course not."

"Good." Amelia ran her hand lightly over the blue silk gown. "Mr Alexander Fenbridge will certainly find you lovely wearing this."

Lottie smiled. "Alex tells me I am lovely even if I am dressed in my oldest clothes."

"Why would you possibly wear your old outfits when you have beautiful new ones?" She caught Lottie's sigh and belatedly added, "but that is most affectionate and romantic of him."

"One day Mr Brightford will shock you by managing to say something romantic."

"If he did it would probably be when I had just taken a sip of wine and I would cough and splutter all over him. I doubt we will ever manage a conversation where we do not disagree over something and quarrel."

"Does that not alarm you?" Lottie asked with a worried expression.

Amelia thought about it. She could see her friend's point but then Amelia had never been one to enjoy a quiet existence. She was happier arguing with Mr Brightford than she was being paid compliments by any other man. "As long as he managed to kiss me between quarrels I believe I would be content."

* * *

Mr Brightford tried to be polite to his hostess and her daughter while keeping one eye upon the door of the drawing room. When Amelia arrived with her mother and aunt he grinned with relief, somewhat startling the two ladies he was talking to. He excused himself the moment she paused in greeting people to fetch a glass of lemonade and walked over to her.

"I am delighted to see you here tonight."

"Congratulations," Amelia said to him brightly. "That is the best first line you have said to me since we met."

"Er, thank you. I wanted to say…"

"Ah, Miss Daventry," their hostess, Mrs Henton said, stepping between them, "I must introduce Lord Connell to you and your mother. He is new to Edinburgh…"

Mrs Henton continued talking as she led Miss Daventry away.

Alex strolled over to him. "How did your conversation with Miss Daventry go?"

"Conversation? I barely managed to say two words to her before we were interrupted."

Alex sighed and shook his head. "You must do better than that."

Brightford glowered at him. "Should you not be inflicting your company upon your wife?"

Alex turned to look at that lady, his expression melting into a smile. "Just so." He wandered off towards her.

Brightford made a mental note that if he died before managing to wed Miss Daventry he must leave all his worldly possessions to his far more likeable and deserving cousin, Nathan.

He kept an eye on the young lady and when he saw that Miss Daventry was finally alone he hurried across the room to her. "I will speak quickly before Mrs Henton finds us again…"

A butler appeared in the doorway and announced dinner.

Brightford fought not to swear aloud.

"Perhaps you should speak concisely too," Miss Daventry suggested as the people began to rearrange themselves into couples by rank for the formal procession down to the dining room.

"Indeed," he said and did so, "I have to leave the city tomorrow on estate business but should not be gone more than two days at most. On my return may I request a private interview with you?"

Miss Daventry's escort appeared to lead her in to dinner and Brightford was forced to find the lady he must walk with ahead of Miss Daventry. They reached the table where Miss Daventry's seat proved to be on the far opposite side to his. He watched desperately as she took a seat, then she looked up and caught his eye.

She nodded.

CHAPTER THIRTY-FOUR

"MISS DAVENTRY, there is a gentleman who is requesting to speak to you alone," the butler said in a disapproving tone.

Amelia's heart leapt: Mr Brightford must have managed to conclude his business more quickly than he had expected. She threw down her embroidery, jumped up and headed to the door.

Before she could escape Mrs Gallerton objected: "Who is this gentleman? It should be for your mother to decide whether you may speak to him unchaperoned."

"I am certain Mr Brightford's request is not in any way improper." She attempted to leave but it was the butler who, to her surprise, stopped her this time by clearing his throat in a meaningful manner. "Yes, Williams?"

"My apologies for not speaking more clearly, Miss. The gentleman waiting in the drawing room is the Duke of Elborough."

Amelia glanced downwards as she composed her expression to hide her disappointment and surprise. She hoped her mother and aunt would not pounce on the fact that Amelia had expected to be requested to have a private audience with Mr Brightford.

"Who is the Duke of Elborough?" Mrs Gallerton asked, clearly impressed by the title.

"A gentleman I am quite sure I do not want Amelia speaking to alone," Mrs Daventry said.

Amelia grimaced. "I hardly wish it either but I do not see that we can get rid of him otherwise."

"Will one of you tell me who this man is?" her aunt insisted.

"The Duke tried to make Amelia an offer last year but her father said she was too young. He is widely regarded as dangerous and cruel."

Williams looked with uncertainty at the ladies and Amelia made the decision for herself. "Thank you, Williams. If the Duke wishes to speak to me then of course I will see him. Mama, I believe you will require my company in about five minutes?"

"Quite right, dear," Mrs Daventry said, "and do not allow him to intimidate you."

Amelia nodded and walked into the drawing room, hoping that the matter was not what she feared, although she could not imagine what else he could want to speak to her about privately. The Duke bowed to her, the smile he wore doing nothing to improve his ill-favoured features.

"Good morning, sir. You must understand that my mother does not allow me to speak to gentlemen unchaperoned except in the most exceptional circumstances."

"Naturally," he agreed, "but I believe she could have no objection to what I wish to say to you."

Amelia suspected that he could not be more wrong in this belief. "Then would you have a seat, Your Grace?"

He gestured for her to sit first and, when she had done so, he followed suit. "Miss Daventry, I have admired you since your coming out last year. Your beauty, innocence and grace are beyond compare, although I fear I am not the kind of loquacious gentleman who can speak poetically on such matters…"

Thank goodness! She tried to get in a word but he was off again before she could manage it.

"… I trust you will think no less of me for speaking plainly. I wish you to do me the honour of marrying me. It will allow you to take your place at the head of society as you deserve and I will be a generous husband…"

He was certainly not lacking in confidence, behaving as if her acceptance of him was a foregone conclusion. "Your Grace, I am rendered almost speechless by this offer from such an important member of society as yourself. However, I regret that I must turn you down."

He stared at her as if he could not understand her words. "If it is a matter of obtaining your mother's permission to marry you…"

"No, sir, it is not. I fear I cannot marry a man I do not love."

His expression grew darker and she felt uneasy. "Perhaps you are too young to understand the honour I do you in making this offer."

"Not at all. I am highly flattered, but I fear that does not change my answer."

He bowed to her and swept out of the room without another word.

Amelia gave a shaky sigh. Thank goodness she would never have to speak to him again.

* * *

"You should not have had to see him on your own," Lottie said, shuddering.

"He was a little alarming," Amelia admitted, "but he is still a gentleman. I should think myself exceedingly feeble if I could not turn down a man's offer of marriage without support."

"He is such an unpleasant man…"

"But a wealthy and important one," Amelia said, clearly

trying for a lighter tone. "It does my sense of consequence great good to know I have turned down such a distinguished person."

Lottie gave a reluctant laugh. "At least the matter is out of the way now."

"Indeed."

Before they could continue the conversation a butler came into the drawing room and announced dinner. She and Amelia joined Mrs Daventry and Mrs Gallerton in the dining room.

"Your husband is not joining us?" Mrs Gallerton queried.

"No, there was a talk at the university that he wished to attend."

"I hope your husband is not one of those intellectuals one hears about."

Lottie saw Amelia bite back laughter as many of Edinburgh's titled gentlemen were fellows at Edinburgh University. "Not at all. He simply takes an interest in matters of politics and society."

"Does he have a seat at the House of Lords?"

"No."

"Hmm." Mrs Gallerton looked dissatisfied. "I suppose you have heard that Amelia has turned down yet another offer of marriage?"

"Aunt!" Amelia exclaimed.

"Mrs Gallerton, that remark was uncalled for," Mrs Daventry said. "I explained to you what kind of man the Duke of Elborough is."

"Yes, yes, I intended no criticism."

Lottie was beginning to suspect that the woman said little that was not meant as criticism.

"The fact is that Amelia has not made the impression upon Edinburgh society that one might have wished," Mrs Gallerton said, continuing before the subject of these words could object, "so I intend to give her a second chance in a larger pond."

Lottie saw her own confusion mirrored on the face of her friend and that of Mrs Daventry.

"I wish to take Amelia to London and launch her into the very best society in the world. I do not doubt that she will immediately gain admirers there and perhaps she will finally agree to marry one of them."

CHAPTER THIRTY-FIVE

"DO NOT overwhelm me with gratitude," Mrs Gallerton said at the prolonged silence that followed her suggestion.

"Forgive me for not expressing my appreciation immediately. I know the money and work involved in a coming out in London and never expected such immense generosity," Amelia said. Her aunt looked mollified and pleased with this answer, giving Amelia a chance to consider what to do. She could hardly say that she had every intention of going to London with Mr Brightford and had no need of a coming out ball. She could suggest that she believed he was about to ask her to marry him but she had been wrong before and had been humiliated when she told Lottie and her family that Mr Wrackley was about to propose, then he did not do so, or at least not for several months. She did not doubt Mr Brightford - not exactly - but he might still change his mind or be delayed in asking or any number of things.

No, the only thing she could do was prepare to go to London and hope Mr Brightford truly did love her and would propose before she had to go.

"Where would we stay in London, aunt?"

* * *

Lottie and her husband had luncheon with Mr Brightford the next day.

"It will be pleasant to get home again," Mr Alexander Fenbridge said to his cousin. "We have decided to leave at the end of the week."

"It is a shame that Amelia will be leaving so soon and will not be free to stay with us," Lottie commented to her husband, ignoring the sharp glance from Mr Brightford, then addressing him, "Perhaps you would care to stay with us instead, sir. I am sure Mr Nathaniel Fenbridge and my brother would be happy to see you."

"Where is Miss Daventry going?" Mr Brightford demanded, uncivilly ignoring the rest of her words.

Lottie buttered a scone. "Perhaps I should not say. The matter is really just Amelia's concern, although it is exciting for her."

"Where is she going?" he repeated while her husband watched the two of them with amusement.

Lottie deliberately took a bite of her scone and ate it, while he waited with increasing impatience. "I am surprised that her aunt considers it necessary now that Amelia has received a second offer of marriage."

"What?" Mr Brightford jumped to his feet.

Lottie looked up at him with an expression of innocent enquiry.

Glaring, he sat down again and turned to Alex: "Perhaps you would be willing to tell me what is going on here."

"It is my wife's news."

As two pairs of eyes turned to her again, Lottie took another bite of her scone.

* * *

Six months ago there was nothing Amelia wanted more than a proper coming out in London. She had dreamed of having lovely new outfits for every occasion, of meeting famous people and going to balls every night.

So much had changed since then. Her father had still been alive, Lottie was still living in Edinburgh, and Amelia had not known Mr Brightford at all. She thought now of his intelligence and wit and of his perceptive appreciation of her intelligence and wit. Mr Brightford was perfect for her and surely he had indicated that he felt the same? She remembered in England Lottie saying that she could not wait to begin married life and that was how Amelia felt now: she wanted to kiss Mr Brightford and talk to him every day and live in his house with him.

Six months ago she would have been thrilled to be going to London. Now she only dreaded the thought of being parted from Mr Brightford.

* * *

"Please would you request that I be allowed a private interview with Miss Daventry," Mr Brightford said to her butler. He was not taking another chance of losing her. Elborough of all people. London, he could imagine, would hold far more appeal.

"I am afraid Miss Daventry is not in, sir."

So much for the two hours he had spent this morning trying to think of the best words to convey his desire to marry her. "Are you expecting her back imminently?"

"I fear I do not know of her plans, sir. Do you wish to speak to Mrs Daventry and Mrs Gallerton?"

If Mrs Daventry had been alone he might have chanced making small talk and hoping Miss Daventry would be back soon, but he had no intention of subjecting himself to Mrs Gallerton's curiosity. "No. I will return in an hour or two."

"Yes, sir."

He turned away from the house with a grimace. Now he would have to try and remember his eloquent marriage proposal for another two hours - he was bound to mess it up and it would be just like Miss Daventry to laugh at him.

He smiled to himself at the prospect: as long as she accepted him she could laugh as much as she wished.

* * *

Amelia and her maid emerged from one of Edinburgh's largest milliners then Walker gave a shriek at the same time as Amelia felt herself grabbed. She struggled in the grip of two strange men and tried to tell them that they had made a calamitous error and would suffer the consequences with a jail sentence if not a hanging. Walker was pushing at the men, trying to reach Amelia, but the men shoved her back, knocking her over.

"How dare you!" Amelia exclaimed, fearing Walker had been hurt, then she was thrown inside a carriage in so rough a manner that she nearly fell to the floor. A man's hands reached for her and she tried to pull away, but found herself assisted into a seat, the hands not letting go until she stilled. The vehicle began to move, hurtling down the roads away from the familiar streets and safety.

The carriage curtains had been closed so she could not immediately see anything beyond a figure in the darkness opposite her. He barely looked human and the danger of her situation hit her hard, making it difficult to breathe. It must be a mistake, though: her family had no wealth; no one could have anything to gain in taking her.

She swallowed her fear, glared at the apparition and said, "My name is Miss Daventry and I demand that you return me immediately to where your henchmen found me."

"I know who you are." The man leaned forward and

she went cold as she recognised him, the threat ten times worse than she had feared. This was not, after all, a mistake and there was no one she was more afraid to be alone with. "You are the future Duchess of Elborough."

CHAPTER THIRTY-SIX

MR BRIGHTFORD knocked on the door of the Daventry household and once again informed the butler that he wished to speak to Miss Daventry.

"Er, yes... Would you wait inside, sir?"

He barely noticed the butler's unusual hesitancy, still trying to keep the words of his marriage proposal in some kind of order in his head. He did, however, notice when he was left standing in the entrance hall instead of being taken into the drawing room. The butler opened the door to another room and Brightford could hear the sounds of hysterical voices and... was a woman in there crying?

He took a step forward then stopped himself. If someone was ill or some other misfortune had taken place then it was up to the family if they wanted his assistance. It hit him with a lurching sensation in his stomach that it might well be Miss Daventry who was ill or hurt.

He was left with these disturbing thoughts for only a moment before the butler reappeared and led him into what looked like an informal family living room. It was a maid who was crying and trying to talk at the same time, although she halted, wide-eyed when she saw him.

Mrs Daventry had a haggard look of distress to her but

managed to sound composed as she said to him, "Sir, can we rely upon your absolute discretion for the sake of helping Amelia?"

His fear was proven correct. "Of course. What has happened? What can I do?"

"She has been abducted."

"I beg your pardon?" This was one danger he had not imagined and he could scarcely believe it.

Mrs Daventry turned back to the maid: "You were saying that you recognised the carriage, Walker?"

"Aye, Ma'am." She visibly gulped down a sob. "It was that man who proposed to Miss Amy."

Wrackley? He thought. *No, impossible…* Realisation hit him and it all made sense in the worst way. "The Duke of Elborough."

The maid nodded vigorously. "Aye, him."

"I believe he was angry when Amelia turned down his marriage proposal," Mrs Daventry said in a dead tone and Brightford remembered she had no one left except Miss Daventry.

"You said he was evil but I never would have believed a gentleman could do such a thing," Mrs Gallerton interjected and for once he was grateful she was here and Mrs Daventry would not be alone to cope with this.

"I would believe anything of Elborough." He turned to Mrs Daventry. "I will find your daughter and return her safely to you. You have my word."

* * *

"I have no wish to marry you, sir, and insist on being returned home," Amelia told The Duke of Elborough, as his carriage continued to drive her away from her friends and family and the further away it got the more afraid she became.

"No," he said. Just that. He did not even try to justify

his behaviour.

"You have clearly not considered what you are doing: marriages have to be planned. They do not take place on one man's whim."

"You have not taken the time to know me as I know you. I have planned this in detail: I have a special licence and a vicar is ready to perform the ceremony."

"He cannot do so if the would-be bride refuses to say *I do*."

"You will say it," he told her, but she was not swayed by the iron in his tone, only dismayed at the detail in his plot.

"No."

"You will say it," he repeated, "because after spending a night alone with me you will only be accepted by any member of polite society as my wife."

Amelia clasped her gloved hands together so he would not see how badly they were shaking. By now Walker would be home and would have told her family what had happened. Amelia did not know if Walker had seen who took her, but they must be able to guess that only Elborough had the power and lack of morality necessary to do so. She had no intention of marrying him no matter what the consequences but there was no point in angering him now. Her mother would turn to Mr Brightford and, if she could gain time, he would find her.

"You are right," she said, attempting to sound calm. "It did not occur to me that you had thought this through so thoroughly."

"Indeed," he agreed smugly.

She glanced away from him and the sight that greeted her made her lean against the carriage window, staring out. "This cannot be the way to your home - we are leaving Edinburgh."

"That is right," he said. "After all, we would not want anyone to interrupt our time together, would we?"

How could anyone find her now? Fear rose up in her

again, threatening to overwhelm her, as she thought of what the Duke had planned for her.

* * *

"So, have you finally asked Miss Daventry to marry you?" Alex asked when Brightford arrived at the home of Mrs Fenbridge's parents.

"She is gone."

His tone clearly conveyed his worry as Mrs Fenbridge went still and stared at him with large eyes. "Gone where? What has happened?"

"I know Miss Daventry is your friend, Ma'am, but the only way to save her is for your husband to help me and for you to remain calm, despite what I am going to tell you." When Lottie nodded Brightford said, "The Duke of Elborough has kidnapped Miss Daventry, presumably to force her into marriage."

Lottie put a hand over her mouth, the colour draining from her face, but she did not speak.

Brightford turned to Alex: "I need you to help me find her. Every moment she is alone with him, she is in danger."

Alex nodded then said to Lottie: "Stay with your parents." He touched her cheek. "We will find her."

"The Duke will not behave honourably, to Amelia or to you," Lottie said. "If he gets his hands on a weapon then be very careful. Do whatever you have to do to get her away from him."

It was sensible advice and Alex followed it, collecting his pistol before leaving the house. They headed first to the Duke's home and, not taking the word of the staff that no one was there, Brightford and Alex searched every room.

"Any clue?" Brightford asked as Alex re-joined him downstairs.

"There are signs that Elborough packed a trunk," Alex said in a grim tone.

Brightford heard these words with a tightening around his heart: if Elborough had taken Miss Daventry out of Edinburgh then he had no idea where to look for her. "One of the staff must know something," he said. They had to. Otherwise their task would be an impossible one.

They assembled the household servants in the hall downstairs and Brightford said, "We urgently need to find Miss Daventry, a young lady The Duke of Elborough has abducted. Her reputation and perhaps even her life are at stake."

The group of sixty or more servants looked blankly at him, not one of them showing the least concern or inclination to help him.

He exchanged helpless glances with Alex then a different method of persuasion came to him. He emptied out all the money he had with him. "I will pay for information."

Suddenly everyone had something to say. It seemed that the Duke had managed to hire an entire staff as greedy and heartless as him.

* * *

When the carriage pulled up at a private residence Amelia's last hope of help died. She had been counting on them staying at an inn where she might beg for help. The duke could not have planned this more thoroughly.

As the carriage halted Amelia threw open the door and ran towards a nearby wood. She knew this could be the only chance she got and moved as quickly as she was able but after less than a dozen steps Elborough caught her. He held her in a painful over-familiar grip as he forced her back the way she had come and into the house. Once inside he let her go.

A woman - presumably a housekeeper - had opened the door for them but had not reacted to the rough way Amelia was being treated.

"We will have dinner in two hours," Elborough said to her and she curtsied and left. He turned back to Amelia: "I will show you to a room where you may compose yourself. I expect you to behave in a more ladylike manner from now on."

He sounded angry about her escape attempt and for a moment her own temper rose up and blotted out her fear: did he think she would meekly accept being forced into marriage to him? She remained silent as he gestured for her to ascend the staircase and as she began walking she could hear him right behind her, like some predator stalking her. She imagined having to live the rest of her life with him and knew she would be better off dead than enduring his attentions.

* * *

Mr Brightford strode from Elborough's home, Alex beside him. They had the name of the house the Duke had rented under an alias. Now, since it was in the countryside far beyond the city, they had to find it. Time was running out for Miss Daventry: every moment she was alone with Elborough he could be hurting her in a way she might never recover from.

Brightford had once seen Elborough shoot a horse for not winning him a race. He remembered the expression on Elborough's face and the thought of his having Miss Daventry at his mercy became even worse. The Duke had no conscience to stop him taking what he wanted from her.

"We must hurry," he said as he reached his horse and mounted the gelding. "We have to find them before nightfall."

"Indeed," Alex responded, jumping into the saddle on his own horse. "Her reputation would be destroyed if she spent a night alone with him. That is clearly what he is counting on."

"I do not care about her reputation - I will marry her the moment she agrees to it - but I cannot allow him to harm her."

They galloped off into the waning day.

CHAPTER THIRTY-SEVEN

AMELIA HEARD the door being locked behind her and she immediately ran to the window and pulled it open. She grimaced at the sight of the long drop below her and wondered if the situation had become desperate enough as to make it worth risking breaking her neck. If she was lucky and avoided that, she would likely break a leg and still be unable to escape. No, she would have to hope that a better means of freeing herself presented itself during the evening. She deliberately did not dwell on what she would do if she managed to get outside - it would be better to be alone in the middle of nowhere than here with the Duke.

There was a jug of water, bowl and towel on the table at the end of the four-poster bed so she cleaned and tidied herself the best she could with no mirror or change of clothes. She was waiting impatiently when the door was unlocked.

She swept out of the room the moment the door opened, having no wish to be alone in a bedroom with Elborough.

He looked her over in his usual unpleasant manner then held out her arm for her to take so he could lead her down to dinner. "Shall we?"

She glared at him, refusing to play along with the game that nothing was wrong, and marched downstairs ahead of him, not hurrying but keeping an eye on the front door. Her heart fell and her anger rose when she saw a footman standing guard in front of the door. That was her main means of escape blocked, she realised, panic growing.

She pushed down her fear and followed the scent of food to a small dining room, lit only by several candles. Places had been set at either end of the oak dining table so she sat down and the Duke, entering the room just behind her, sat opposite. A servant - the woman who had let them into the house - served them soup then left.

"I trust you are in a more gracious mood now you have had time to compose yourself and consider the many advantages of your position as my wife," Elborough said, picking up his spoon, and the gall of his words made her lose her temper.

"Had I the slightest wish to be your wife, I would have accepted the proposal you made me," she told him. "If you believe you can induce affection by kidnapping me then you are far more feeble-minded than I ever imagined."

He dropped his spoon with a clatter and his expression was so violent that she feared he would hurt her. She clenched her hands into fists, letting the nails bite into her palms so she would not do something pointless, like screaming, and his expression slowly calmed.

"By this time tomorrow you will be my wife," he said, breathing harshly. "You will learn to obey me and to treat me with respect one way or another."

He returned to his soup and she did the same, her hand shaking as she picked up the spoon, hoping the meal would stop any further conversation between them. After what felt like a lifetime the next course of their dinner was brought in a served to them but she felt too sick by now to do more than pick at it.

"You are not drinking your wine," Elborough

commented.

"It has an odd taste," she lied as a new means of escape occurred to her. "I do not think the glass was washed properly."

He paused a moment, frowning and she held her breath. "I will fetch you another," he said.

He left the room and she jumped up and hurried to the window. It was stiff but she managed to get it open, only to hear Elborough's returning footsteps. He must have only gone to a room nearby. She looked helplessly from the window to the door, paralysed by the thought of what he might do if he caught her.

She saw a statue on the sideboard. She hesitated, uncertain whether this new plan would work, but she only had seconds left so she ran to it and picked it up - it was as heavy as it looked. She positioned herself behind the door and bit her lip, waiting, the statue a dead weight in her arms.

The door opened and Elborough stepped inside, a fresh glass in one hand. He saw the open window and stopped just in front of Amelia, who was concealed from his sight by the door. She hefted the statue up and brought it down hard on his head. He fell to the floor with a satisfying thump that she hoped would leave him with bruises and a headache. She let the statue drop to the floor then straightened and pushed the door shut, to stop the staff realising what had happened.

Amelia ran to the window.

* * *

Brightford and Alex stopped in front of a manor house and got down from their horses. This must be the right place. He could only hope for the thousandth time that they had got here early enough to prevent any harm befalling Miss Daventry.

"Mr Brightford!"

He recognised the voice but could barely believe it when he saw Miss Daventry running over the grass to him from the side of the building. He caught her in his arms and she held onto him tightly, shaking, as he closed his eyes, the hours he had spent fearing for her well-being finally over. They must be married quickly as he never wanted to leave her alone again. As he embraced her he said, "Where is Elborough? How did you escape?"

"I bashed him over the head with a statue," she told him breathlessly but with distinct satisfaction.

At these words he laughed, pride welling up at the realisation that she had bested her kidnapper. "And we thought you might need rescuing!"

She pulled back from him and he reluctantly let go of her. She caught sight of Alex and smiled at him then looked back at Brightford with a solemn expression, "I promise, I have never been so grateful to see anyone ..."

The front door of the house opened and Elborough and two men ran out, all coming to a halt when they saw Brightford and Alex. They all assessed each other and, out of the corner of his eye, he saw Alex reach for his gun.

"How did you find us?" Elborough demanded, looking ready to tear them apart for ruining his plans.

"That hardly matters now. Miss Daventry is safe and if you ever so much as speak to her again I will kill you," Brightford promised.

"Then I will give you the chance to do so," Elborough said with a smile that promised vengeance. "I challenge you to a duel."

"No!" Amelia exclaimed.

"I accept," Brightford said.

"No, you cannot." Amelia grabbed his arm, paler than ever.

"I will have my valet send you details of the time and place." Elborough gave Amelia a look that suggested things were not over between them but, before Brightford could object, the Duke turned and strode back into the house.

Amelia's hand was still on his arm and she looked up at him with far more terror than she had shown for her own sake. "Do you not see that he wants to kill you to deny us the chance for future happiness together?"

He knew what Elborough intended but there was no other solution. "The Duke is a danger to everyone around him. I have to stop him."

CHAPTER THIRTY-EIGHT

WHEN AMELIA saw her mother again she burst into tears. She felt a fool about it but it was as if half the fear from her capture was only hitting her now and, on top of that, she was now frightened beyond words for Mr Brightford's life.

"You are safe now, my dear," Mrs Daventry said, holding her and patting her back as if she were a child again who had had a nightmare. "It is all over now."

But it was not a harmless dream and it was not over: she was safe but the man she loved was not and she knew she had to find a way to stop Mr Brightford and the Duke fighting each other.

It was the middle of the night by now so, after the explanation of all that had happened, Mr Brightford left and Amelia asked for a bathtub to be brought up to her room. While the necessary water was being heated and pails of it were carried upstairs it came to her what she must do. It was in fact something Mr Brightford and Mr Alexander Fenbridge had said about the Duke of Elborough's staff that provided the answer. They would betray him if offered enough money.

She sent for McGillis, one of her family's footmen, and

gave him her orders. He did not look happy about them but nodded and left.

After that she took her bath, scrubbing the day's events from her body, and then she was finally able to relax.

* * *

Lottie was not concentrating on her breakfast or even on her beloved husband. She was still in a state of shock over what had happened to Amelia and needed to see her as soon as possible to check that Amelia was unharmed and not too distressed over everything.

She hardly spared a glance when Mr Brightford's butler entered the dining room and held out a tray with a card on it to him. "This was left for you, sir."

"Thank you, Mills."

"What is it?" Alex asked.

Mr Brightford read what was on the back of the card then tossed it down on the table and continued with his breakfast. "I will be seeing the Duke of Elborough again tomorrow and it will be the last thing he does."

The words, only half listened to, did not immediately make sense to Lottie but her husband's subsequent silence had an ominous feel to it and she repeated in her head what Mr Brightford had said. A duel, Lottie realised, vividly remembering the fear her entire family had suffered when Benjy had fought one. "If you love Amelia and your family then you cannot do this. If you die we will all be left to mourn and if you succeed and kill him you will have to flee the country or be executed for murder."

"My wife is right," Alex said. "There is no good outcome to such an action."

"Perhaps not," Mr Brightford said, "but I have no alternative. The Duke is a danger to Amelia as long as he is alive and her safety is more important than anything else to me."

Lottie listened to this, all appetite gone, as she thought how Alex and Amelia would feel if Mr Brightford were to die. The Duke of Elborough had found a way to wreck their lives after all.

* * *

"I have the information you wanted, Miss Daventry." The footman stood awkwardly in the doorway to Amelia's bedroom, Walker glowering at him for the impropriety of his being there, despite the fact he was only obeying Amelia's instructions.

"And you told Mr Brightford's butler the wrong time?"

"Aye, Miss. I told him to get there an hour later, as you said."

"Excellent. So where and when did the Duke of Elborough's man say the duel would take place?"

He gave her the instructions but exchanged worried looks with Walker as he did so. She could not have all her work undone now so she told him firmly, "You have done well, McGillis, and have probably just saved a good man's life."

His frown faded and he nodded to her and left.

As soon as he was gone her maid said, "Miss Amelia, what are you planning? After what you've just escaped, I won't let you go anywhere without me."

"Then you may be reassured," she said. "You, McGillis and Darrow will all be accompanying me tomorrow morning."

Walker failed to look the least bit reassured. "And where will we be going, Miss?"

Amelia decided to save that fact for the last minute and wondered what was the best outfit to wear to a duel.

* * *

Brightford got dressed at the appointed hour and found Alex waiting for him downstairs with a long face, ready to act as his second in the duel. He took no satisfaction in what lay ahead; indeed, given that he had seen what an excellent shot Elborough was, he could have no certainty of surviving beyond the next hour. However, he was certain that Elborough would not give up on his obsession with Miss Daventry; if he could not marry her then, given the chance, he would find a way to harm her.

"Alex, if Elborough should kill me, will you promise to look after Miss Daventry? Elborough might try again to force her into marriage if I am not there."

"I promise." Alex put a hand on his shoulder. He had tried to talk Brightford out of this last night and, after getting nowhere, seemed resigned but his worry showed in his eyes. "As long as you will promise to do your best not to let that happen."

"Happily." He put more confidence into his tone than he felt. "I have a strong desire to wed and I do not want to let down the lady in question."

He thought of Miss Daventry as they left the house, hoping that, whatever the outcome today, she would be safe for the rest of her life.

* * *

Elborough's expression was almost amusing when he saw Amelia, rather than Mr Brightford, emerge from the carriage.

"What are you doing here?" he demanded, walking up to her, his presence bringing back all the fear she had endured during her abduction.

Amelia felt McGillis step closer to her. He had a gun of his own with him, which reassured her that the Duke could not threaten her again. He could, of course, kill her but she was counting on his twisted feelings for her preventing this. "I am here to fight a duel," she said. "Can someone explain the rules to me?"

"This is ludicrous," Elborough's second – a man she did not recognise – said.

"Where is Brightford?" the Duke asked and his expression made Amelia have to, once again, reassure herself that she was safe before she could answer him.

"He is not here and I am. Your only chance of a victory today is against me. Now where are the duelling pistols and what should I do?"

Elborough explained the rules, ignoring the heated objections from his friend and from Amelia's servants. The duel began and, as Amelia took the required twenty paces away from the Duke, she wondered if this was in fact as good a plan as it had seemed last night. He had wanted to marry her. He could not shoot her. Could he?

Amelia turned, pointed the gun about a foot above Elborough's head and shot. The gun jolted her backwards and she fell to the ground just as another shot sounded. She looked behind her and saw the bullet embedded in a nearby tree at chest height. She stared at it in disbelief then turned to the Duke, who was walking towards her, McGillis and Walker also running over the grass to her side. Elborough held out a hand to help her up, which she ignored, demanding, "Were you aiming for my heart?"

He gave a shrug. "It seemed appropriate."

She got to her feet on her own as a familiar carriage came into view and pulled up near to the group, Mr Brightford and Mr Alexander Fenbridge emerging from it and taking in the scene.

"What is going on?" Mr Brightford asked, moving to her side. "Miss Daventry, why are you here? Are you hurt?"

"I am well," she said, brushing twigs and leaves from the back of her pelisse, then added in a light tone she did not feel, "I just fought a duel and nearly died."

Brightford was still staring at her, as if unable to

comprehend the words, when she took his arm and looked back at the Duke of Elborough. "Should you ever meet a woman who shows the slightest inclination towards marrying you," she told him, "I will be waiting to inform her of exactly what manner of reptile you truly are."

CHAPTER THIRTY-NINE

MR BRIGHTFORD stood opposite Amelia in the drawing room the next day, the curtains open and letting in a golden glow of autumnal sun. He got down on one knee. "Miss Daventry, would you...?"

"Yes," she said at once, feeling as if she had been waiting for this moment for most of her life.

He looked up at her with a frown: "I have an entire speech prepared with compliments and a rhyme."

A rhyme? Mr Brightford? This she must hear. "Excuse me, sir. Pray, continue."

"With your hair as dark as night and eyes like a sunny morning sky, you fill all the hours of my world ..."

"That is beautiful," she said, smiling at the thought of him sitting composing a speech for her.

"Alex helped with the day and night simile."

"You are both very talented."

"You would make..." He hesitated and frowned. "I have forgotten the next part."

"Was it along the lines of '*will you marry me*'?"

Amusement glinted in his eyes as he looked up at her. "It was an extremely long-winded but elegant version of that."

"Then my answer, Mr Brightford, is yes."

He got up a little awkwardly and she caught his hand to steady him. He held onto it and put his other arm round her waist.

Feeling a bit breathless at his proximity and the feelings his touch provoked, she said, "Should you recall more of the compliments later do tell me."

"I have the whole thing written down at home." His hand was warm against hers and he stroked her fingers.

She swallowed. "I look forward to your recitation."

He kissed her and she put her arms around his neck, holding onto him, as the world dissolved into the most delightful sensations. It was better than anything she had known and it occurred to her that she had a lifetime of such kisses ahead of her.

As she opened her eyes she gazed at his beloved face and said, "About that rhyme..."

Thanks for reading!

If you enjoyed this novel please consider leaving a review on Amazon or Goodreads as this really helps independent authors in getting our books known. Thanks very much.

Free Book

If you would like to get a free copy of my story **A Lively Christmas Season**, a sequel to **Complications**, and find out about my upcoming novels and special offers, sign up for my e-mail newsletter at my website: http://clarejayne.com.

ABOUT THE AUTHOR

Clare Jayne began writing novels nearly three decades ago, when she was a teenager. She has worked in a variety of jobs, including legal secretary and sales advisor, while continuing to write and trying and failing to get a traditional publisher for her work. She has had a short play performed by the local amateur dramatics group and recorded on local radio and came joint first place in a local writing competition. This inspired her to self-publish and she is thrilled to be able to finally share her novels with actual real people.

58265988R00128

Made in the USA
Charleston, SC
06 July 2016